FALLEN DOW

~ Book

S.M PHILLIPS

To
My Dixie,

Love you lots.
DPhillips
♡ xx

~ PLAYLIST ~

~Passenger– Let her go
~Coldplay– Fix you
~Boyce Avenue – Find me
~Paloma Faith – Only love can hurt like this
~Sam Smith – Lay me down
~Ella Henderson – Beautifully Unfinished
~Goo Goo Dolls –Iris
~Paloma Faith – Picking up the pieces
~Christina Aguilera – Say something

BOOKS BY S.M PHILLIPS:

ESCAPE DOWN UNDER (Down Under #1)
FALLEN DOWN UNDER (Down Under #2)

OBSESSION (Obsession #1)

To my boys,

Words cannot describe how happy you both make me

PROLOGUE

"What the fuck was that?" I say as soon as the lift doors close before me. "Are you out of your goddamn, fucking mind? Shit, Stella." I wipe the taste of her away from my lips with the back of my hand, as the image of Jess stood before me tears me up inside. Just knowing that she has witnessed Stella kissing me, makes me see red. Especially after I have just experienced the pain that was written all over her face.

"I thought it was what you wanted. Hey, I'm sorry Max." At least she has the decency to look like she means it. Does she even know that Jess saw? Of course she fucking does. Fuck. I only came to the office to catch a break, to make sure Jess was okay without actually having to see, or talk to her. Then Stella arrived, and it all went to fucking shit. What am I even still doing here? I should be running after her, trying to make her understand, that what she actually saw, wasn't what it looked like. Who the hell am I kidding, like she's going to believe that line.

"Why would she believe me?" I laugh out loud to myself. The last guy she was with lied to her and look how that panned out. Maybe it's for the best. At least this way she can hate me, and I can try and rest easy knowing that the reason she hates me wasn't done intentionally. "How could you think that's what I wanted? Fuck, I'm sorry if you feel that way, really I am." Have I made her feel like I want to be involved with her? I made my feelings around Jess pretty goddamn clear, so why would she think I was coming on to her? This is getting pretty fucked up, and fast. Me and Stella have been friends for years, that's all we have ever been and I never expected her to want more.

"Maybe I should go, unless you want me to stay?" She asks, innocently.

"Nah, I think enough damage has been done for one day, don't you?"

"I can't imagine what Jess must be thinking right now."

"Don't you fucking dare, Stella." I snap as my fist connects to my desk. I feel nothing but a pure heated rage take over my entire body, as I think of all the scenarios that must be flying around that beautiful little head of hers.

"I can go after her, maybe explain what actually happened?"

"Again, are you fucking crazy? She's just walked in and seen us together, and you want to go and talk to her?" Fucking hell, Stella must have a death wish. I might not have known Jess for very long, but what I do know is that she doesn't take any prisoners. "I'll sort it. How about we forget this ever happened? Maybe it's best you leave for the day, hey?"

"You sure? I don't think you should be left on your own, right now." I watch as she eyes me filling my tumbler with some whiskey, but to be brutally honest, at this moment in time, I couldn't give a fucking toss what she thinks, or anyone else for that matter.

MAX

"No, please Max. Please make them stop, I don't want to go. Don't let them take me, Max. You promised you would never leave me." The sound of her voice breaks my heart. Knowing that there is nothing I can do to stop it from happening, breaks me, kills me a little more on the inside. Another knife to the heart, just in case we haven't suffered enough. The only decent thing that I have left in my life is about to me ripped from within my reach, and there's not a fucking thing that I can do about it. I try to shout, to let her know I can hear her, but no sound comes out. All I can see is her tear stained face, as the car drives away from me.

I suddenly jolt awake, my emotions are on edge and my body is covered in a sheen of cold sweat. The last image in my mind still hovers at the surface. Big, sad, brown eyes filled with tears as she is taken away from me. Running my hands through my hair, I try to collect myself. "*It was just a dream Max.*" I repeat over and over to myself. Shit, I haven't had a dream like that for years. Maybe I should cut back on the whiskey if it's triggering old wounds to open. The last thing I need right now, is trying to cope with that crazy shit going around and around in my head constantly. I slowly lift myself out of bed, nausea coming and going in waves, with each breath that I take. Seriously, it was just a dream. I thought I was over all of that pussy arse shit, obviously not. The house feels quiet, and if I'm being honest, it no longer feels like home without Jess' presence. She doesn't deserve to be treated the way that I've treated her. I know I've been a complete bastard, but it's for her own good. She's better off without me in her life; I just need to make sure that she's okay. No matter how I do it, I'll make sure that I find a way.

"So you finally decided to wake up, old man?" I say as I walk through the open door in front of me.

"Max!" Daisy shouts, as she jumps up from her chair and dives into my arms. As I look at her, I can see relief swimming in her eyes. It's so fucking good to see Mal awake. Sure he'll have to take it easy for a while, but he's here and he's alive, that's all that matters.

"I'm beginning to wish I hadn't, son. My head's pounding and the sight of you is making it worse. What the hell happened to you?" Jeez, he's been out of it for weeks and all he can do, is ask how I am. Some things never change.

"How about you start worrying about yourself from now on?" I don't even need to turn and look at Daisy, to know that she's rolling her eyes. The day Mal decides to care about himself above all others, would be like seeing a kid without sweets on Halloween.

"When can I get out of here? I've been going insane."

"When the doctor says so dear, and no sooner." I watch them both, and can't help but feel like I am back in my teenage years. Daisy has always worn the trousers in their relationship. Not in a bad way either, she's always kept him on his toes that's for sure.

It's been a shocking couple of weeks to say the least. Mal flew out as a surprise, after being held up, back at

Stanton's. It turns out, he developed a blood clot on the flight over, which then resulted in a heart attack. As soon as he was admitted to the hospital, they carried out some tests which lead to surgery. As if he hadn't put us through the mill enough, he then went and had a reaction to the anesthesia and landed himself up in intensive care. But Mal had decided he wasn't quite finished with the worry and stress just yet, and had a another heart attack two days later, only this time he fell into a coma.

"I think you made your arrival known Mal, now it's time to do as you're told. You hear me?" The grin he flashes back at me signals that he has heard me, loud and fucking clear. But that doesn't mean to say he's going to act on it.

"Oh Max, you know he isn't going to listen to you, dear. He hasn't listened to me in almost three and a half decades. Why would he see the point in starting now?" Daisy has a valid point as usual, all the while, Mal continues to grin at us both from where he's lay in his hospital bed.

"Well, I'll let you get your lunch and I'll come back to see you this evening. Daisy, if you need anything, just let me know and I can make sure that I bring it up later." I hate having to leave them at the hospital. I hate that there is nothing that I can do. Waiting is a fucking bitch. The sooner he's out of here, the better; for all of us.

JESS

"He's on the mend, so it's definitely good news."

"That's great to hear. We've all been worried sick. Bloody hell, he's always been so healthy, too. To say it was a shock, doesn't even cut it."

"Apparently it can happen to anyone, at any time. Even the fittest of people too. I'm just happy that he's finally awake. Poor Daisy's never left his side, not once."

"That's true love for you, princess. Any idea when you're likely to be coming home? It's been too long already. Please tell me you'll be back for your birthday?" She pleads. I can hear Jen's heels clicking around in the background as we have our daily catch up. I can just picture her now, pacing her living room like a mad woman. She always does, when something is outside of her control.

"God I hope so, I'm not really a fan of spending it alone." Saying it out loud pains me much more than keeping it on the inside, where only I know how much I have left myself down. Allowing myself to fall for someone when I knew, just knew, straight from the off, that this is where I would end up. One of these days, I'm sure I'll eventually learn my lesson.

"Oh princess, have you not spoken to him yet? He seemed pretty into you when he was over here."

"Things obviously change, Jen." I didn't even want to talk about Max and once again here he is, always appearing when I want to forget about him. "I'm pretty sure he's occupied with other stuff right now, anyway."

"Talk to him, please? You could be pushing away a really good thing, all because of your stubbornness and your goddamn pride."

"You didn't see them together, Jen. She's obviously wanted to get her claws into him for some time. I guess seeing how he was with me made her up her game, some." I knew there was a reason why I hated that bitch as soon as I heard her voice a mere few weeks back. I'd love nothing more than to give her a right good slap, but the professional in me is far too strong.

"Well for what it's worth, I think you'd be stupid not to try." I can't help the laugh that escapes me, at her *wise* words of wisdom.

"You would. I'm not as bold as you Jen; I shy away from rejection like a fucking recluse on the tube. I let my barriers drop and look how well that turned out."

"You know I'm not going to let this drop. Anyway, this bitch needs some sleep, so I'll call your stubborn arse later."

"No worries, good night and I love you."

"Love you too princess."

I place my phone back onto the table, feeling a little homesick. What I would give to walk into Joe's with Jen and George for a bloody good piss up, right now. I throw my head back and welcome the glorious heat as it shines down on me. Maybe Jen's right. What if it was a misunderstanding?

"Yeah right." I say aloud, to myself. If that was the case, what's stopped him from calling me to explain? Nothing, absolutely, fucking, nothing. Which tells me he's just like the rest of them, fucking arse.

"Talking to yourself again?"

"It soothes my mind." I reply, opening one eye to look at Melissa. I still feel pretty awkward staying here. After all, she is Max's sister and I don't think she's had much experience taking in his strays before. It's not exactly the ideal situation, but I don't really have anywhere else to go and she was kind enough to offer me a room and I'd hate to offend her.

"Hey, as long as you're happy, then that's all that matters right?"

"Yeah, I guess." I smile up at her, while the ache in my chest weighs me down.

"Shit, I'm so sorry. Completely the wrong thing to say."

"Don't worry about it, I'm good, honest. I'm glad you're back actually. I've been meaning to talk to you."

"Finally decided to let your hair down and have some fun with me, then?" She says hopefully. Melissa has been hounding me since I moved in with her to go out and have some fun. It's all well and good to plaster on a fake smile, god I've been doing that for most of my life, but when you throw alcohol into the mix, shit could get embarrassing. I don't want to be the one that spills their heart out while drunk, least of all with Melissa, which is exactly what I will end up doing. I don't think she'd appreciate me telling her all about how much I need Max in my life.

"Maybe." I say to stall the begging that will come later. "But that's not what I wanted to talk to you about." Shit, how am I going to say this without sounding like an ungrateful cow, especially after everything that she has done for me?

"Spill it then, woman." She demands. Sometimes she acts just like her brother and that's pretty hard for me to handle, even though it's not her fault. It does however give me the push that I need to continue.

"I'm going back to London." There, I've said it. Taking a deep breath, I mentally give myself a high five. I wait as Melissa just looks at me, yet she doesn't say a word.

Now I definitely feel like an ungrateful cow.

"I'm not following you." She says after quite a long pause. Her eyes focus on mine and I'm a little too scared to answer her. Angry Melissa isn't someone that I really want to mess with.

"I'm going back home, Liss." I say, silently praying that this conversation will soon come to an end.

"I'm not that stupid Jess. I know what you said, what I don't understand is why?" Wow, really. Did she actually just say that? Isn't it pretty fucking obvious?

"Well, now that Mal's on the mend, I don't see any reason for me to be here. What with everything that has happened anyway." I say the last part more quietly, because knowing my luck, if I say it out loud, somehow Max will hear me and suddenly appear.

"Bullshit. Have you even spoken to my brother? Have you even let him explain his side? Believe what you want Jess, but I'm telling you now, he would never go for Stella in a million fucking years."

"To be honest, I don't feel comfortable here anymore, Liss. It's not you, it's me." I stop after realising what words have just come out of my mouth and we both burst out laughing at the same time.

"Did you really just quote a breaking up speech at me? In case you didn't know, I have a vagina. Unless you're into that kind of thing. That would be pretty funny actually as it would prove that Max doesn't actually have any balls."

"I'm not even going there with you, Liss. I'd just be happier at home, I guess. All the project work can be done from Stanton's anyway." I feel really bad as I'm trying to explain how I feel to her, and also defend my actions too, but I know I need to get it all off my chest.

"Well you know best, but please speak to him before you go. You don't want to look back later on down the line with a bunch of what ifs following you for the rest of your life, and I really can't be arsed with having to deal with him pining after what could have been. Do you know how miserable that would make me?"

"Sure." I nod knowing full well that I won't be contacting Max in the slightest. The sooner I'm back on home turf the better. I'm bloody miserable myself. I have been, ever since I witnessed them both in their passionate embrace. I guess I'd rather be miserable, instead of playing the fool though. I've already had the pleasure of experiencing how that feels. I lower my sunglasses as Melissa steps back into the house; just in time to hide the hot, salty tears of defeat that begin to fall.

Max

"You know she's leaving right?"

"I'm busy right now, Liss. Can this not wait until later?" Fucking hell, why does she do this? She comes barging into my office without a care in the fucking world, just to get her point across. I could have a boardroom full of clients and she wouldn't bat an eyelid.

"Did you even hear what I just said? She's leaving, as in, going back home to *England*. Don't even tell me that you're not bothered, Max. I know she means something to you. I know that she is starting to mean fucking everything to you."

"How many times do I have to tell you to back the fuck away?"

"What is wrong with you? Oh my god. It's true isn't it? You're actually with Stella. Max you can't be fucking serious?" She squeals.

"No. I am not with Stella, never have and never will be. Listen, what Jess saw was a complete misunderstanding"

"Why haven't you told her that, then? She's going to hop on that plane and she will be gone, straight out of your life, as if she never existed. Is that really what you want?" I have to collect myself before I answer her. Shit, when did my sister give a crap about who I was with?

"Listen to me, Liss. It's for the best that she goes. Nothing good can come from her staying here. If she stays, she'll only end up resenting me and I'm sure she can do that from home, without having to see me every fucking day."

"You seriously need your fucking head checking, Max. She's the best thing that has ever happened to you, and you're just going to let her walk away, and leave her with an impression of you that isn't true?"

"Leave it Liss." I stand and stare straight at her. She's as stubborn as me. It's pointless trying to explain it to her, she wouldn't get it, anyway.

"You could at least have the decency to apologise to her. She's out here on her own, and the only people that she knows aren't around to comfort her, because one's in hospital and the other one has well and truly fucked her over and is the cause of all this pain in the first place. Do me a favour? Get your fucking shit together and fast. You're acting like a spoilt fucking brat and it doesn't suit you one little bit." She's so sure that she knows what she's talking about, it's pointless trying to argue with her, so I leave her to storm out of my house without saying a word. What the fuck is this? Everyone take a chunk out of Max week? Jeez, I preferred it when my life was more laid back.

"Your dinner's in the oven, dear." I hear Martha down the hall before she enters my office.

"Thank you." At least someone's against giving me too much of a hard time. My stomach grumbles at the mention of food, and I can't actually remember the last time I ate anything. "Why don't you give yourself the day off tomorrow? You've been here an awful lot, this past week. I don't fancy getting sued for making you ill."

"What, and leave you wallowing here on your own? Don't be so silly, Max."

"I'm just busy, that's all. You really don't need to worry about me." All I want is for people to stop fussing over me, like I'm a kid that can't fend for myself.

"Max." She says softly, as she sits down opposite me,

a maternal look present in her eyes. "I've known you an awfully long time, and I would like to think you had a little bit more respect for me, than to actually lie to my face."

"Honestly, I'm fine. I've just got a lot going on, that's all." In a sense, I'm technically not lying to her. I can't remember the last time my head was filled with so much bullshit.

"Have you spoken to her? Have you made sure that you've told her your version of events?"

"Wow, seriously? Does everyone seem to know every fucking detail of my personal life, now?" I snap unintentionally at her and instantly feel like shit for it. When did I become so goddamn fucking interesting?

"Stella stopped by looking for Jess. She said that there had been a misunderstanding of some sort and she wanted to talk to her. It doesn't take a genius to work out what actually happened, dear. To be honest, I've never liked that Stella from the get go, but I normally like to keep my opinions to myself." The sudden pressure that fills my head causes my fingers to shoot straight to my temples. Fuck this bullshit. As if sensing my sudden unease, Martha continues "Don't worry, I didn't tell her where she was. That poor girl doesn't need any more drama and I personally will not be responsible for any further damage that whirlwind of a woman will cause."

"She's leaving anyway, so what does it matter?" I can't fucking believe that those words have just left my mouth. I can't think of anything worse than the thought of Jess being permanently out of my life, but I swore to myself I wouldn't be selfish with my needs when it comes to her and her safety. I've witnessed more than enough people get hurt because of me, and if anything happened to Jess, I honestly don't think I could live with myself.

"Do you want her to go?" Martha asks the question as if it's the most simplest thing to answer in the world. If only it was that fucking easy.

"What do you think?" I finally ask her after a pause. "It would be so much easier for her to walk away now, before any more damage can be done. But will it be easy for me to watch? Hell no."

"If you want my advice, go and talk to her. Try and tell her how you feel, regardless of that male ego of yours. Just promise me something, don't turn your back on a good thing. Jess is your good thing, Max. Whatever you do, don't lose it."

Jess

The hospital still makes me feel sick to my stomach. The smells, the association of death, pain, everything you don't want to be around, is closed in, all around you under one roof. I'm on edge every time I'm in a hospital and I can't wait to get out and jump in the shower to scrub the feel and smell away.

"Hey you. How are you feeling?" I ask, leaning into Mal and placing a tender kiss on his cheek. He looks so much better, especially now that all of his wires have been removed. The last time I saw him, his face was still grey, yet now he has a healthy glow and he's rocking some rosy cheeks and a sparkle in his eyes. "I take it they've been treating you well, then?"

"Like you wouldn't believe, flower." Knowing Mal, I bet he's had these poor nurses at his beck and call, at every bloody opportunity. I can't help but laugh at him, my chest suddenly feels so much lighter now that I know he's going to be okay. It's one thing Melissa giving me updates, but seeing him face to face makes it all feel more real.

"So what's the plan from here, then?" I'm still a little unsure as to what's happening with Mal once he's been discharged. A pang of guilt creeps in for not coming to see him more often, while he's been here. My reasons aren't that valid either, only to me, for being the selfish bitch that I am. I didn't come to see him because I was scared that I would bump into Max. Yep, definitely a selfish bitch.

"Well, it's looking pretty good for them to discharge me soon." A huge smile lights up his whole face, which instantly fills me with a sense of happiness. "I can't wait to stretch these bad boys, let me tell you."

Daisy walks in, just as I wipe away the happy tears that have made a run for it. It's so bloody good to have him back.

"Jess dear. It's so good to see you. Has Mal told you the good news? Honestly," she sighs, "I can't tell you how relieved I am. Getting him to rest is going to be the tricky part."

I watch them, as their faces light up at the thought of finally being free from this place, and how in love they still look after all these years. Now definitely isn't the time to drop my bombshell. I stay with them for a little while, laughing and joking as if everything is how it should be, and right in this moment, I don't have to worry about anything but the three of us in this room.

I step out into the sunshine, my eyes squinting from the sudden change in brightness. I struggle to see for a moment, until my eyes slowly adjust. I take a few steps forward and my heart contracts as soon as I see the most beautiful sight before me. I stand motionless, unable to put one foot in front of the other, completely transfixed on him. My eyes never leave his, as he watches me intently. His look alone has me feeling weak at the knees. Clearly, neither of us expected to bump into each other. He slowly steps towards me and then stops just inches away from me. His mouth opens and closes a few times, as he decides whether or not he's going to say what he was going to say.

"Hey." He says, a shy grin curving his mouth into that cocky grin that I miss so bloody much. Not that I'd ever tell him, though.

"Hi." I reply, feeling rather awkward. After all I have done to prevent this meeting from happening, yet here he is, stood in front of me, acting as if nothing has happened. "It's great news that Mal's on the mend." I say, trying my best not to look at him straight on. Whenever I do, it's as if he can see straight through me and into my soul. I step backwards, so that I can get away from him, as it all suddenly becomes too much.

"Jess, wait. Can we talk?"

"About what?" I reply, pretending I don't care, just to see if he will make a comment about Stella.

"I've not seen you much at the office. I thought you had meetings scheduled all week?"

"I did, however I postponed them until further notice. You've got access to my calendar, so surely you could have checked that? Why don't you see if Stella can fit them in, seeing as she's your current employee of the month?" Childish remark? Maybe, but fuck if I care. He doesn't say anything back to me. He just stands here, his face remaining impassive as he watches me stare him down. "Do you know what, whatever Max. I'm done." I turn to head in the opposite direction, more sure now, that going home is the best move of them all.

How could I be so stupid to think that I could be different to all the other women who have been and gone before me? So we've fucked more than once, big deal - it obviously doesn't have to mean anything. The sooner I'm away from him, the better. I'm pulled back suddenly as big, strong, powerful hands secure my wrists so I can't break away.

"Stop fucking running, Jess. Jesus Christ, woman, will you fucking stop?"

"Do me a favour and leave me alone, Max." I plead, knowing full well that he won't, but it's all I want him to do, right now. It's too painful to be around him. How can he not see that?

"I can't, goddamnit. No matter how much I try, I just can't get you out of my fucking head." His words cause me to look up into his deep, pleading blue eyes and I start to soften towards him, my heart trying it break free once again. All too soon, I see a massive haze of auburn hair getting closer and closer in the distance. All my walls sharply shoot back up, just as fast as they came crashing down, at the sound of that high pitched voice. She's bloody everywhere.

"Max, what's taking you so long?" Her mouth forms a perfect O as soon as she sees that it's me who has his attention and holding him up. I pull my hand out of his grasp, now that it has slackened somewhat at the interruption of the Queen bitch, and I almost whack it against the car door next to me. I don't doubt for a second, that she would love nothing more than to witness me walking back into the hospital with an injury.

"Fucking hell, Jess. Will you just hear me out?" His voice is demanding as he stares me down.

"It looks to me, like you're pretty busy already. I'll see you around, Max." If ever I needed further proof that they were together, today has set it in stone. Why else would she be here? I'm so fucking angry. Angry at myself and angry because I know right now, that they'll both be laughing at little old me. I knew all along I'd be the laughing stock. I guess I've only got myself to blame once again, for not going off my initial gut instinct.

The sun begins to set as I look out over the horizon. The sight really is beautiful. There's something calming about the sound of the waves crashing against the shore and watching them ripple as the sky prepares for darkness to fall, as it says goodbye to another day. I sit here and allow my mind to wander on its own account. Nothing matters while I'm sat here. Nothing but the feeling of peace that takes over my body All of the drama that has suddenly attached itself to my life takes a backseat while I'm here, in my new found happy place. Here, I don't have to meet any expectations. Here, I can feel what I want to feel without worrying about getting hurt, or not being good enough. I'm not sure how long I have been sat here, all I know is that it's slowly getting dark and the chill is beginning to set in.

One question that I have asked repeatedly to myself today is, do I really want to give up on all of this? Do I really want to give this once in a lifetime opportunity up, because of some guy? I guess he's not just *some* guy though. It would be so easy, much too easy, for me to hop onto the next plane and head home, but that would only benefit and please one person. *The Queen, fucking bitch.*

I miss Jen and George so much, but I'll get to see them when I get home after I have finished this project. Coming back here won't be as easy the second time around. So what if I have to face Max and Stella eventually. Sure it will stab at my chest like crazy, but now Mal's out of hospital and I'm sure he won't mind me working away from the office. I'm sure I can pop over and keep him entertained from time to time, too while I'm at it.

I get up and dust the sand from my arse, my decision made and set firmly in my mind. Why should I give up this once in a lifetime opportunity, before I have to? Jen would only stick my stubborn backside on the next flight back over here anyway, and all that would have resulted in, would be a massive dent in my credit card. Why the hell does my life have to be so goddamn complicated?

I look behind me and see the dim glow of lights coming from Melissa's. She must have arrived back from her travels without me noticing. I've no idea how she will react at the news that she's going to have to deal with my mopey arse self for a little bit longer. I guess I'm going to find out soon enough.

I place my bag on top of the island, as I step through the kitchen and look around me.

"Liss, you home?" I shout out, but I get no reply. It's pretty quiet, surely she's home if the lights are on? Or maybe she has some posh automatic ones, the ones that come on with one of those fancy timers. Oh well, I guess my little announcement will have to wait until tomorrow. Looks like a shower and an early night with my kindle is in order, and I'm quite excited at the thought of it. I almost jump out of my skin, when I see a sudden movement in the living area. I stand stock still on the spot, unsure how I am going to react to this intruder. I don't even have a weapon. Fuck, fuck, fuck. As the figure gets closer, I notice that the intruder is male, quite well built and almost naked. *What the fuck*.

The closer he gets, the more I can make out of the person coming towards me. With my heart still hammering in my chest, I breathe in a sigh of relief.

"Um hi." I manage to force the words to leave my lips, my eyes still lingering on the bunched up cloth that's just about covering his manhood.

"Shit, sorry Jess. I didn't hear you come back." I look to Melissa and take in her sheepish expression as she dashes through to the kitchen. The poor love, I've never known anyone look so embarrassed.

"Hey, you don't need to apologise. It's your house after all. Plus, don't look so scared, I knew you two were shagging right from the off." I can't help but grin as her mouth goes slack with shock.

"You did?" they both say in unison.

"Erm, yeah. It was pretty obvious, the way you two were drooling over each other and everything. Wait... Max doesn't know does he?" I ask, but have a suspicion that I'm already going to know the answer.

"Are you fucking crazy, lady? He'd put my mother fucking balls through the ringer for even thinking about Melissa like that." He's really not bullshitting. He looks absolutely petrified. It's actually quite comical to watch and I can't help but laugh. He stands in front of me, bearing his tall, lean muscular frame, yet he looks like a little boy who has been caught out doing something that he shouldn't have been doing.

"Well, he's definitely not going to be hearing it from me, that's for sure." I mumble. I don't realise that they both heard me, until I see them both hang their heads at the same time, unsure what to say.

"Jess..." Melissa starts to say but I cut her off by holding both of my hands up.

"You two randy dogs, go and stick some clothes on. While you obviously do it for each other, you're doing absolutely nothing for me. I'll stick the kettle on if anyone fancies a brew." I give them one last smile as I walk back towards the kitchen and I'm one hundred percent positive that the image of Heath will remain etched into my mind for quite some time, possibly locked away for the next time I feel intimidated by him.

Max

I hear shouting in the distance and instantly know that he's home. Fear and dread wriggle at the bottom of my stomach. I cover my ears to try and drown out the noise, praying that it will stop, but it's no good. All I ever hear is him shouting, constantly from the minute he gets in until the moment that he leaves again. My mother never says anything to him when he shouts at her, and when I ask, all she says is "*Daddy needs to vent every now and again honey. When he gets home your daddy's tired from working all day. He doesn't mean to upset anyone, sweetie.*"

It doesn't matter what she says, or how many times she says it, I don't like it. Not one little bit. Mummy never shouts and she cleans all day, cooks and makes sure all of our school work is done; yet she never raises her voice, not once, not even to *him*. It's not nice when he shouts at my mummy.

As his voice gets louder and louder from the next room, I look towards the other side of my bedroom and see that Melissa is still fast asleep. It makes me so angry that she's going to grow up around this. No one should have to witness stuff like this, especially not Melissa. Fortunately, she's too young to understand. At the delicate age of five, hopefully she will forget. It's not too bad for me, because with time I will grow bigger and I'll be able to stand up to him and stop him from hurting us, ever again.

A knock sounds at my door pulling my mind out of

the past. Shit, I really need to get my head together. Either that, or it's looking more likely that I'm going to have to give Don a call. I slowly lift my head up from within my hands and see Daisy patiently waiting to come in. What the hell is she doing here at the office? Shouldn't she be at home looking after Mal? Fuck, Mal. I mentally pray that she isn't here to tell me that he's been taken ill again. When I look at her though, I'm relieved to see her smiling. If Mal was ill again, she definitely wouldn't be smiling.

"Hey, what are you doing here?" I ask as I pull the door open for her to come inside my office.

"I just thought I'd stop by and bring you some lunch. You look like you could do with a decent meal. Maybe you can tell me what's been getting you so down lately?"

"I'm good, but thanks for the offer, I really appreciate it." Do I really look so fucking bad, that Daisy feels like she has to turn up and look after me? Her husband is at home, recovering from his near death encounter and yet here she is, making sure that I'm okay. "How's the old man settling in?"

"Perfectly dear, just like we expected him to. He's much better now that he's no longer cooped up in that hospital bed all day. I left him catching up with the sports, while I quickly run some errands. To be honest with you, I think he'll be glad of the peace and quiet. Apparently I'm mothering him too much."

"Is that wise? You know how worked up he gets watching stuff like that..."

"Max dear, by all means, you can go and try telling him no. I'd love to watch his reaction." I laugh knowing that she has a pretty valid point. The stubborn streak that Mal has, must be hereditary. We both use it pretty fucking well.

"Would you like a drink?" I want to get to the bottom

of why she's really here, and fast. It has to be something important to pull her away from Mal's bedside.

"Oh yes dear, that would be lovely, thank you. Tea, two for me."

"Spill it, then. Tell me why you're really here." I say. It's pointless trying to beat around the bush with her, it just makes her angry, so I always have to get straight to the point with her.

Daisy eyes me intently and I begin to feel slightly uncomfortable. I suddenly regret asking that question. Now I know where this is going. I should have fucking known.

"I'm worried about you Max. Is there anything wrong with that? I want to know what's happened to you. Mal's out of hospital and on the mend, yet you look just as frightened and fragile, as the little boy that you were all those years ago, and do not try to tell me that nothing is eating away at you. I know you better than you would like to admit, Maxwell." One thing about Daisy is that I have never been able to hide shit from her, ever.

"I guess I'm still dealing with the shock of everything that happened with Mal. It was scary shit, Daisy. Surely you can understand that. It was like everything was happening all over again and there was nothing that I could do to control it."

"Yes, but he's home now. He's safe and nothing bad is going to happen to him, so please, stop worrying. Now, what about Jess? Where is she? I haven't seen you two together for a while." Bingo… and this is what she wants.

There's no way in hell that I'm discussing this with her. I knew that she'd bring it up eventually. She doesn't miss a fucking trick. What the fuck am I supposed to say to that anyway? Admit what an absolute bell end I was. Shit, still am, by pushing her away and punishing her for something that she can't control?

"She's staying with Liss, that's all I know." That's all I say. It's not my place to tell Mal and Daisy that she's going back to London. The thought of her leaving, tears me up inside and fills me with a burning rage. Its better this way, I remind myself before I lash out again.

"I think I might just stop by Melissa's place and see how they are both getting on. Whatever it is that's bothering you Max, don't let it eat away at you. You've been down that road before, we all have and none of us want you to experience that again. Whatever it is, nip it at the bud and soon. You know you can always talk to me, don't you?."

She's right. Fuck, she's always right. I need to find a way to get past this. I've done it before, so I can do it again. It looks like that call to Don is becoming more and more appealing every second of the goddamn day. As soon as Daisy has finished her tea and made her reasons for stopping by known, she is soon on her merry way, to finish her errands. Before she leaves, she updates me on Mal and his latest demands, damn he's milking this for all it's worth. But he's here and he is alive, so it really doesn't matter and man, doesn't he know it.

The office before me still remains empty. I can't bring myself to step into Jess' office. As silly and pussy like as it sounds, I don't want anything to be touched. I want everything to remain as she left it. Shit, I sound like she's fucking died. Maybe it's for the best that she's going back to London. At least then, she will be out of my way and I won't be able to hurt her any more than I already have. Running my hands through my hair, I let out a frustrated sigh. Why does she get to me this way? No one has ever gotten to me like this before. Jess fucking Townsend. A woman of fucking mystery.

Jess

"I'm so, so sorry about last night Jess. Please don't think I make a habit out of bringing people back here all the time, because that couldn't be any further from the truth." I eye Melissa over my morning coffee as she sheepishly sits before me.

"Why are you apologising to me? It's your house, Liss; you can do what the hell you like. Shag the whole of Australia for all I care, you really don't need my permission." I laugh.

"I'm so embarrassed though. I guess I'm that used to having my own space, I just didn't think about you coming back. I can't bear the thought of what could have happened if you had been Max."

"Seriously, it's okay. Get some coffee down you and quit apologising." I say as I pour her a cup. "One thing I don't get, and please tell me to butt out if needs be, but why are you hiding all of this from Max, anyway?"

"Are you kidding me?" she squeaks. "He'd kill him; actually kill him, that's why. Best friend or not, he'd chop his fucking dick off. You think you have witnessed Max being overprotective? Well you ain't seen shit yet, girly."

Okay, so not exactly the response I was hoping for, but I can understand her predicament. "So it's just a bit of fun with you two, then?"

"I really wish it was. It would be so much easier if we just met up for some casual sex every once in a while. Shit Jess, what can I tell you? I've been in love with Heath, ever since I can remember. Hitting on your best friends sister is one thing, but you're openly asking for a death wish if it's Max's little sister. Trust me. It wasn't easy growing up with him weighing up every guy that I spoke to."

"That's pretty shit, on the plus side I'm glad it's not just me who he feels he can try and control." I smile at her, while thanking my lucky stars that I never had an older brother who thought it was his place to interfere. On the other hand, it's also pretty sweet and it proves that yes, Max does actually care about the ones who are close to him.

"That's just it Jess, don't you see? He's only ever been overprotective and controlling with me."

"Well I guess that's because you're his little sister and he wants to look out for you, make sure that you're okay, it's only natural. There's nothing wrong with that really. You'd be asking yourself some pretty deep questions if he didn't bother with you. All you need to do is ask him to back off a bit if he gets too much. If you don't tell him that it bothers you, then he will never know, will he?"

"Yeah, I hear what you're saying, but what I meant was, he's only ever acted like that towards me, until *you* walked into his life. Everything you have just said to me, now applies to you, too. He really cares about you, Jess. Anyone who can't see that must be a fool, including you. He's just too fucking stubborn to admit it."

I try to ignore her questioning look but she wins and stares me down. *Bitch*.

"I'm not into this let's change the subject game. How long have you and Heath been living in sin, then?" I'm a complete hypocrite I know, but I desperately need to change the subject myself. I'm really not all that comfortable with where it seems to be heading.

"Well, like I said. I've loved him forever. From a

distance anyway. I guess I should thank you, really."

"Me?" I ask, utterly confused.

"Yes, you. While Max was in England, pretty occupied with you by the sounds of things, he had Heath keeping tabs on me to make sure I was okay. Like I said, he's pretty overprotective with me. He started to come around at first to see if I needed help with anything, and then before I knew it, he was taking me to work and then picking me back up as soon as I had finished. I'd be lying if I said it didn't make me feel special. Shit, I didn't even need to worry about Max breathing down my neck every five minutes, either. It was pure bliss.Then a couple of nights later, one thing led to another." She smiles a wicked grin as she continues, "we've been pretty much inseparable ever since."

"I like seeing you smile like that. It makes your eyes dance." I say. She really is beautiful. No wonder Max didn't want guys coming into her life and taking advantage of her. If she was my little sister, I think I would act the same way.

"Do you know what would make me smile even wider…?"

"Not so fast Melissa Wild. I'm sorry to have to break it to you, but it looks like you'll be sad for a quite some time."

Today is a new day. Today is the day I get my balls back and stop moping about like a wounded little puppy. So what if Max is now with Stella? I'd like to think that it's more his loss, but I doubt he'll be losing any sleep over it. I'm going to use everything I have to be the bigger person here. It might hurt a little. Who am I bloody kidding, of course it's going to hurt, a lot, but Mal trusted me with this project and I aim to complete it, with or without Max by my side. One thing I have never been is a quitter and I don't plan on changing that anytime soon. Now it's time for me to enjoy myself and relax while I'm here. It's not as if I will be coming back again, once my work here is complete. I never used to get worked up about such small things and it's driving me bloody crazy. With a newly acquired dress fresh out of Melissa's wardrobe, I brush myself down and gear myself up for the day ahead, whatever it may bring.

My heart drops a little as I exit the lift on the fifteenth floor. My eyes automatically fix on the door in front of me. Images of the last time that I was stood here, flicker in my mind's eye and cause a dull ache to flood through my chest. I take in a deep breath as I step forward. Knowing that I am alone makes it a little bit more bearable. I'm not entirely sure how I will react to Stella when I see her. As long as she doesn't provoke me, I'm sure I can keep it professional, or at least I'll try my best given the circumstances. It's no surprise that the reception desk is once again, empty. What the fuck does Stella do most of the day? Scrap that, I actually don't want to think about what she's doing – or should I say *who* she's currently doing? After all this time I'm still yet to find out who my assistant is. Thank god it's not the queen bitch. I really don't think I could handle that.

As soon as I enter my office, it doesn't skip my attention that everything is exactly how I left it. As I step towards my desk, I notice that my diary is still wide open where I left it. Jen and George are looking up at me as if nothing has changed, but oh, how it fucking has. Since I was here last, I have had my heart ripped out and stomped over, my boss having a much too close a brush with death and a horrific bout of homesickness that encased me so much so, that I am amazed I could even breathe. I guess they say that these things are sent to try us and they make us stronger.

Once I have settled in and my coffee is where it should be, in my hands ready to fuel me for the day, I start the joyous task of tackling my emails. No sooner have I opened them, Jen's beautiful face pops up on my screen. Normally I wouldn't answer her calls at work, but seeing as no one is around I accept the video call. Who doesn't enjoy being a rebel every once in a while? Plus, familiar faces and surroundings always make me feel better too.

"Hey, hey, hey." She chirps down the screen at me. I laugh, tears of both happiness and sadness filling my eyes as they try to make a break for freedom. I miss her so bloody much.

"Hey yourself." It feels so good to hear her voice. Looking at her surroundings it seems that she is at home. "What's new?"

"Nothing much princess. Just thought I'd check in on you and see how you are doing. What's happening with you?" I sigh a little and I know she doesn't miss it, especially as she can see my face.

"I'd love to tell you everything was hunky-bloody-dory, but I'd be lying through my teeth. Things are okay, I guess I shouldn't be moaning really."

"Oh, so are you talking to Mr Mystery yet?"

"God no. But, I've decided that I'm not going to get myself down about it, either. What's the point? I'm here to do a job, not mope about how much of a stupid cow I've been. I need to enjoy this experience as much as I can, otherwise I will end up regretting it and then I'll only beat myself up about it."

"That's my girl." She laughs.

"The best way to look at it, no matter where I am; I will be dealing with a dickhead whether I am at home or away, so what does it matter?"

"Oh I love what you did there, princess. How far behind are we on the episodes? I hate having to sit down and watch it without you."

"Do you know, I haven't even checked. I don't want to know what I have missed, as I'm so far behind already." Me, Jen and George always settled down to watch the Home and Away Omnibus every weekend without fail. I bet the little sods have been watching it without me though.

"Hey, erm... I understand why if you haven't told me, but has Josh tried to call you while you've been over there doing your thing?" Jen asks me, with a weird expression on her face.

"No. Why would he call me? I made it perfectly clear when I last spoke to him that he had no reason to contact me, whatsoever." Why would she be asking if Josh has called me?

"It's just that he's been hovering around Stanton's recently. Apparently, George has spotted him a couple of times. He must be waiting for you to come back, or something."

"He doesn't even know that I left, well he didn't do. I guess it doesn't take a genius to work out that I'm not around though. I'll give him a call later and see what his game is."

"Don't bother yourself with it princess, George said he'll have a word if he sees him again anyway." She says in her reassuring tone, while twirling her glorious hair between her fingers. I guess it looks like today isn't going to be as positive as I initially thought. Why would Josh be hanging around Stanton's? More importantly, why would he keep coming back when he clearly knows that I'm not there?

"What's the update on you and lover boy?" A huge grin spreads across her face which convinces me that things are still rocking in Jen's world and I'm glad too. She deserves to be happy.

"Hey Jess. Still looking good, I see."

"Shit!" I jump in my seat as Luke's face appears before me. Trust Jen to FaceTime me when she has her fuck-buddy around. I'm glad they're both wearing clothes; I guess I should be thankful to her for sparing me that sight. I suddenly feel my face heat up, as I remember what he witnessed a few weeks ago. I'm never going to feel comfortable around Luke again. Ever.

"Um, hi Luke. So are you guys practically attached at the genitalia these days, or what?"

"There's no need to be jealous, sugar tits." Luke howls out at me. No fucking way did he just call me sugar tits? I look at Jen, hoping she'll have something to say in my defence, but instead she's too busy snorting through her laughter. The more time that passes, the more dislike I feel for him. Yes, it maybe because of my own stupidity and embarrassment but still, the guy's a tool.

I'm about to say my goodbyes when I glance up and see Stella heading towards Max's office.

"Fuck, fuck, fuck." I shout, completely forgetting I still have an audience.

"Hey, what's up? Has hot stuff finally decided to tell me he can't live without me and that's he's destined to give me babies?"

"That fucking cow's just shown up hasn't she, so I guess he won't be far behind." I say, choosing not to take her bait. "Listen, I'm gonna have to shoot. I'll call you later and give you the lowdown. Luke, by the way, just so you know, you're an absolute twat."

"Love you…." Jen manages to say before I shut down the call. So much for me grabbing my balls and getting on with things. I feel sick, physically sick. Even my full fat cappuccino and pan au chocolate are no longer doing things for me like they were just moments before.

"Oh hi. Jess isn't it?" How fucking childish? She's what, in her late twenties, maybe early thirties and she's pretending she doesn't remember my name? Yeah, very grown up love.

"Hey, how are you?" My fake smile is plastered on, when all I want to is rip her bloody throat out. I watch silently as she pulls the chair out in front of me and sits down. It looks like she's gearing herself up for a right good natter. What an absolute psycho.

"I'm great, but I'm sure you already know that. I must say, I'm pretty surprised to see you here to be honest. Max told me you were going back to London. I thought you would have left by now." A smirk curls onto her face as she eyes me with her devils snare.

I don't believe I have just heard the words that have come out of her mouth. He did what? So not only am I a laughing stock, I'm now the subject of their pillow talk. Fucking brilliant.

"I don't blame you, not at all. It's only natural that you'd want to go home now that there is nothing here for you."

"Really? What makes you think there is nothing here for me? I'm here to work on this project. Yes work, Stella. Do you even know what that is?" I say a lot more calmer than I am actually feeling right now.

"Don't you feel a little bit awkward?" She asks, completely ignoring my insulting question. "I'm pretty sure I would, especially seeing who you have to work with. You should never mix business with pleasure unless you're one hundred percent sure that they're actually into you, otherwise it could get a little embarrassing." The smile plastered on her face is begging to be wiped off with my fist. I'm about to reply when my phone vibrates on the desk in front of me. I quickly tear my eyes away from the vile creature that's currently sitting before me, and glance at my phone.

We really need to talk. ASAP. Max
.

    No we don't. Not unless it's about work, then I don't plan on talking to him anytime soon. I feel Stella's intense gaze burning into me. Why, oh why is she still here?

    "What do you want Stella? I'm guessing it's not for idle chit chat?"

    "Oh, I don't want anything. I just wondered what you were still doing here. I already have everything I need, but you already witnessed that with your own eyes, didn't you?" I'm thankful for the buzzing of my phone as once again it distracts me from reaching over and slapping that smug fucking look off her plastic face. I know who it is, so I let it ring off. Having Stella witnessing my slanging match isn't going to do me any favours here.

    "Well it's been a pleasure as always." I say, heavy on the sarcasm. "I've got quite a lot of work to do, something I highly doubt you have ever had to worry about, and I guess I need to return these missed calls from Max too. Is there anything else that I can help you with?" The colour instantly drains from her face. Bloody good. She clearly wasn't expecting Max to call me, to be honest neither was I, but her reaction is utterly priceless. Gone is the sure-headed bitch that was sat opposite me a few moments before, instead since I have been here I have never once known her to move on her heels so fast. Jess one – queen bitch Nil.

I haven't got the foggiest idea what Max wants to talk to me about so badly. In the past half an hour I've had thirty two missed calls from him and numerous messages and voicemails, demanding me to answer him. He really needs to understand that he is no longer in a position to call the shots. After a while, I decide that I have kept him waiting long enough and there is no way that I'll get everything done that needs to be done if he keeps disturbing me every two seconds. Plus, if I want to work here and act like nothing has happened between us, then I suppose I need to speak to him at some point. Speaking to him over the phone is a bit more than I can handle right now, instead I settle on sending him an email. I've got to keep it professional and all that jazz, haven't I?

Hi, Sorry I missed your calls; I've been busy working on the development. If you have any problems then I'll be sure to let Mal know as soon as he's feeling up to it. Everything seems to be on schedule so far. If I need anything then I'll arrange it directly through Mal.
Jess

I re-read it a dozen times before hitting send. Why is it so goddamn hard to send an email to him? An email that is strictly professional. I thought I was made of stronger stuff than this, obviously not. By midday, I'm pretty happy with my progress. All the materials have been chosen and ordered and the plans have been finalised. It looks like this little beauty is about to be born and I couldn't be happier with the results.

Now it's time to get some food into my grumbling stomach. I wait for the lift to come back up and as soon as the lift doors open, he's there. Standing tall in all his beauty, Max Wild stares back at me. His eyes lock on to mine instantly and time stands still. As much as I want to, I can't find the strength to avert my eyes away from him, or to take a step back. Instead, I stand facing him with my mouth wide open unable to release the words that try to come out.

"Jess." He whispers. His tone sounds pained, yet he looks very calm and collected. Oh how I have missed his face, his body... how I have missed *him*.

"We need to talk. If you're not prepared to talk to me, fine. But you will listen to what I have to say. Do you understand me?" He now leans over me as I struggle to step backwards. I can feel his body brush against mine and it does all things kind of crazy to me.

"I'm just heading off out to Lunch." I say in a rush. Being this close to him has me confused. I want to slap him so hard, yet I want to devour him at the same time. My head hurts from it all. I know I should be telling him to fuck off, but it's so much harder than I originally thought it would be. The hold he has over me is unreal. What's happened to me, and where has my willpower gone?

"My Office... NOW!" His voice echo's across the empty floor and sends shivers up my spine. Oh yes, I'm definitely in trouble when I'm around him, but somehow this time, I manage to stand my ground.

"I'm pretty busy, but I'll try to catch up with you later." In seconds his face comes crashing down and his lips hungrily seek mine. It takes me a few moments to realise what's happening, and all of my senses fully awaken with his touch and my hands, betraying me on all levels, automatically slide up his solid muscular chest. The heat burns from within him and I respond to his touch as easily as the last time. Once my hands have reached their destination, they flex through his hair as I am forced backwards against the wall. The feel of his body against mine is welcome and a moan escapes my lips, my body desperate for more. My phone begins to ring, bringing me back to reality with a massive bang.

"Don't even think about answering it." He growls as he rests his forehead against mine, his breath coming in short rasps. "We've got stuff to discuss and you're going to listen to me whether you like it or not, lady." His words instantly get my back up. Who does he think he is, barging in here and giving out his orders?

"I'll do what the hell I like. Don't think you can come in here and start dictating what I will and will not do. That's my decision and my decision alone." Hastily grabbing the phone out of my bag, I keep my eyes focused on his so he can see how pissed off I really am. I'd say he was pretty pissed off too judging by the way his jaw is tensed.

"Hello."

"Jess. Where are you? I've got the cocktails in. You better hurry your arse up, because they're evaporating in this heat."

"I'll be with you in five. Did you think to order any food, or is this strictly a liquid lunch?" I ask, but this is Melissa we are talking about here.

"Don't ask silly questions, girly. Just get your backside here ASAP." Before I have a chance to reply the call disconnects.

"Can you and your sister get any more fucking demanding?" I shout at him in utter frustration. I press the button behind me and to my relief it opens straight away. I waste no time in jumping in to get away from his overwhelming presence and the effect he has on me. Max doesn't follow me, which I am more than happy about. Instead he promises, "I'll be waiting."

"You'll be waiting a pretty long time, pal." I say to myself. I don't know if it's nerves or just me being pure childish, but I flip him the bird just before the doors close and I feel pretty damn good about it. What an absolute twatbag. I can't believe I let myself submit to him once again. The guy is unreal, even now I know that he's with Stella, he's still playing his silly little games. I'm such a glutton for punishment when I'm around him. Maybe working from Liss or Mal's, isn't such a bad thing after all.

Less than five minutes have gone by and a Cadillac slows down beside me. I know it's Max without even turning my head to see.

"Get in the goddamn car." His voice is raised and I lose my battle and turn my head to the side to look at him. Oh boy, he's pissed, all right. Even his hands are white at the knuckles from clenching the steering wheel too hard.

"Why are you doing this to me, Max?" I plead. "What is it exactly, that you are trying to achieve with this?"

"Jess, for fuck sake, get in the goddamn car. All I want to do is explain. If you don't get in, trust me when I say I will drag you in here kicking and screaming if I have too and I don't give a shit what the passers-by will think, either."

Honestly, I'm not ready to talk to him. I don't want to hear about him and Stella and how they have decided to work things out. If that's what he's come here for, then he's more of a bell end than I originally thought. I'm also petrified of how I will react to him. He clearly knows he has this strong pull over me. Will he continually try to hound me if I don't get in the car? I make a mental note to grab some wine for tonight, when I will most likely be drowning my sorrows for the pain that I am going to put myself in. I stop and turn towards the car. Oh well, I guess it's best to get this over and done with. Plus, it's a free ride to the beach hut so I'll get to Liss much quicker. Here goes nothing.

Once I'm safely clipped in, I wait for the slow hum of the engine to start back up, but it doesn't. Instead the car is filled with an awkward silence and I can feel Max's stare burning straight into me as if demanding me to look at him.

"I think you need to head that way." I point straight ahead, giving him the hint to move. Instead he just continues to watch me, leaning back slightly into his seat so that one arm rests on the wheel while the other snakes around the back rest of my seat. I steal a quick glance and he looks so fucking perfect. My body is screaming out to be touched by him, but my head knows that it's so, so wrong. If things hadn't have worked out the way they have, right about now I would be sitting in those arms and potentially doing some naughty, naughty things. But unfortunately, shit happens. Why did I bloody get in the car?

"Because you're a bloody silly cow, that's why." I think to myself.

"Max, I'm not interested in your silly little games. Either say what you want to say, otherwise I'll get out of this car and keep walking. To be honest, I haven't got the time, or the patience to be dealing with your bollocks."

Max

It takes every ounce of strength that I have to keep my hands to myself. All I want is to reach out and touch her. Let her know how I much I have missed her, to tell her that I really need her in my life, to let her know how much she has affected me in the short period of time that I have known her, but I can't. That smart mouth of hers never fucking stops, she's not been in the car for more than five fucking minutes and already she's rhyming of her demands. My senses are filled with everything Jess, vanilla and strawberry. Shit, just sitting next to her in the car has me hard. This morning when I woke up I decided that enough was enough. I needed to talk to Jess one way or another, before she boarded that plane and made her way back home. As much as I want to protect her, I'd hate for us to be on bad terms. Normally I wouldn't give a toss but this is Jess that we're talking about and she deserves some kind of explanation – even if it's not the one that she wants.

She's been running around in my head constantly, since she saw me in that mother fucking situation with Stella. Why did things have to get so complicated? I already knew that she would be at the office today after speaking to Melissa earlier. I didn't have a clue what I was going to say to her, I just knew that I need to say something. I arrived at the hotel pretty early and decided to hit the gym to burn off some stress before facing the angel that will somehow be the death of me. Half an hour on the treadmill usually works a treat every time, but today nothing seemed to be cutting it. After an hour, I gave up and hit the shower. Max Wild giving up.

There's another fucking new one.

The hotel is busier than ever right now, and the expansion's looking better than I ever imagined, something that should make me ecstatic. Yet all I feel is a huge fucking void. Only one thing is going to fill that. Only one thing that I will never be able to keep. Fucking Jess Townsend.

By the time midday rolled around, Jess was still up in her office, so I busied myself looking over the plans. Jess doesn't fuck about when she says she's going to do something. Everything has been ordered, booked in for delivery and the work force set in place. What she fell behind on in these past few weeks, she has more than made up for now.

"Mr Wild." A small delicate voice greets me as I step into the foyer, my thoughts wandering into a place of their own. I watch as the heat flushes her face when I look at her. I normally would have taken that as my cue to have my way with her, but not anymore. I nod politely at her, step around her and head to the lifts. I don't even know what I'm going to say to her. Somehow I don't think "*Jess, you drive me absolutely fucking crazy.*" Is going to cut it.

Yes, I know I have been an absolute twat and for that, I want to genuinely apologise for how I cut her off and treated her when Mal fell ill, but right now the one thing I need to apologise to her for is Stella and me and what she walked into.

I guess it didn't help matters when she saw Stella with me at the hospital. Talk about putting two and two together, but shit. What was I supposed to do? Explain in the goddamn car park that Stella had some Gynae appointment. Guys don't talk about shit like that to anyone, ever. Or at least I don't.

Building up enough courage to cup my balls and

swallow my pride, I made my way up to the fifteenth floor to get this shit over with. I'd probably feel better if she fucking slapped me, or something. It's driving me insane the way she acts like she's so over it, over *us*.

Jess fucking killed me the minute those lift doors opened. All I wanted to do was pull her into my arms and feel her body against mine. When I couldn't hold back anymore I took what I wanted, just like I always do. Fucking Melissa had to choose that moment to call, didn't she? She fucking knew I was coming to talk to her today, as well. Now here I sit, my perfect angel sat by my side, shouting out useless threats if I don't start the engine. I drive or she walks. Over my fucking dead body will she be leaving this car until I have said what I came to say. For once in her life she's going to do as she is fucking told. I rub my hand over my face as I try to think how I'm going to word what I want to say to her. Where the fuck do I start?

"Jess, the way I acted when Mal..." Fuck, that's not where I wanted to start. She watches me intently so I continue "Shit Jess, I acted like such an arse."

"Actually, you acted like a complete twat face. I knew straight away when you came rushing into my office that something was wrong and I instantly knew it had affected you a great deal. That's why I left you to it and didn't try to push you. I get it completely Max."

"You do?" This fucking woman sat before me is too fucking perfect and here I am messing up on all crazy as shit levels. No wonder she's heading back home.

"It's done with Max. Mal's better and that's all that matters. Forget about it, I have." Her words hit me hard in the chest, but I try not to show it. I don't want her to know my weaknesses, Shit. I don't want anyone to know my weaknesses.

"So you and Melissa are becoming quite the pair, hey?" I ask. I need to change the subject. I'm not used to apologising, and I'm not sure I like it all that much. I don't know if I should be happy or worried at how close they are becoming, but at least Melissa finally has a female around to do all that pampering shit with, that girls seem to love so much.

"Well I guess she didn't have much of a choice when I suddenly had nowhere to go." There it is, that gigantic boot to the balls that I knew would come eventually. Sure, I fucking deserve it, but it still fucking hurts.

"Fuck." I slam my hand down on the wheel, hard, and she flinches at the sound. "Jess, you have no idea how shitty I feel about everything that has happened. As soon as Mal arrived, everything went tits up. I know I shouldn't have shut you out the way that I did. I guess it was just my way of protecting you. Now that you're going home, it's only right that I'm honest with you."

We both remain quite for some time, neither one of us taking up the place to speak and I can feel those Bambi eyes of hers, burning into me.

"Before I came back to London I was happy in my every day, day to day life. I could do what I wanted when the fuck I wanted, without a care in the world. I didn't answer to anyone and I fucking liked it that way. Shit. I've looked after myself for as long as I can remember, aside from Mal and Daisy anyway." I stop and watch her, mouth slightly agape as she says nothing, just waits and hangs on to my every mother fucking word. I laugh a little as I continue. "Well that's how it was. Right until you came crashing into my life with that smart arse mouth of yours and turned everything I knew upside fucking down. After a while I found a small piece of me needing you more and more each goddamn day, and it's been driving me insane. You allowed me to forget. Shit, you allowed me to fucking feel again."

"Max." She whispers, her lips trembling slightly. Looking into her eyes I see that tears begin to swim to the lids, desperate to break free. I want to take her in my arms right here, but I need to finish what I have started. If I don't, I'm worried that what I want to say will never be repeated again and I need her to know...

I hold my hand up and stop her as she tries to talk. "That night I left, I couldn't bring myself to admit how much you changed me. I was too scared to admit it. As I watched you sleeping peacefully in my arms, I was too much of a fucking pussy to admit that I had feelings for you. So I did what I do best. I upped and left without a backward glance in the hope that if I ignored you, then these sudden foreign feelings would disappear once and for all."

"Why are you telling me this now? None of it matters anymore, Max." Her voice waivers as her emotions break through that beautiful mouth of hers and it kills me inside knowing that I have done this to her. I'm the one who has crushed her and I'll never be able to truly forgive myself for that.

"I went two days Jess. Two fucking days without seeing you, two days without touching you and I felt like I was about to fucking explode. Deciding that I needed to grow a pair, I checked with Mal to see what time you finished but by that time you'd already left. Then I saw you in that bar with Jen and I knew I wasn't going to leave you there. Not with those fucking vultures undressing what was mine, with their eyes anyway. No fucking way was I going to leave you on your own in that state." I can feel my body getting worked up just remembering the look on their faces. How I didn't punch anyone is a fucking miracle.

"So I can tick fun drunk off my list of amazing qualities, then?" My chest lightens a little as a smile dances across her lips. It's only small, but it's there.

"You're pretty fucking hot when you're drunk, you're pretty fucking hot all the time, but I love how feisty you become when you have alcohol in your system. I guess what I'm trying to say Jess, is that care about you. I care about you like I've never cared about anything or anyone before, and it's scaring the fucking crap out of me. I want to look after you. I want to be the one you moan to when you've had a shit day. I want to be the one you fight with and then make up with. As much as I'm trying my fucking hardest to fight this," I wave my hand between us to exaggerate my point. "It's too fucking painful trying to stay away from you, for both of us." There it is. It's fucking out there and I suddenly begin to panic. Her small smile is gone, her face is slack. Her body is rigid and stiff, as she just looks at me as if I'm about to disappear in to thin air. "Say something, goddamit."

"What about Stella?" She says it with such venom that I want to laugh. No matter what life throws at my perfect fucking angel, she always stays true to herself.

"Fuck Stella. What you saw wasn't what it looked like, and yes I know that sounds like a cliché but it's true."

"Really, you sure about that Max? From what I saw she was practically dry-fucking you. Is that something you guys do for fun over here?"Jeez, she doesn't stop or listen to anything anyone says. I run my hands through my hair in exasperation before continuing. "When Mal ended up in hospital it brought back some pretty dark memories. The only way I knew how to deal with, it was to close myself away from those close to me. After the way I'd treated you by pushing you away, I thought it was for the best, to keep you safe. I went to the office so I could make sure that you were okay, but from a healthy distance. I didn't want to hurt you anymore than I already had. I guess when Stella turned up, she picked up on the fact that I was down and read into things completely wrong. As soon as she leaned into kiss me, I was pretty shocked at first and the moment my brain registered what was happening I pulled back instantly, and that's when I saw you."

"Why now? You've never bothered to tell me any of this before today. It's pretty fucking easy to pick up the phone or stop by your sister's house seeing as you knew I was there?"

"I didn't want to hurt you anymore than I already have, Jess. Do you not understand what I'm saying to you?"

"How is telling me going to hurt me more than you already have, Max? That's insane. Instead you've lead me to believe that you and Stella having been laughing at me behind my back. Now that, that hurts more than anything."

"So I did fucking wrong. I told you I'm no good at this shit. The bottom line is; everyone who comes close to me always ends up getting hurt. First there was my mum, then Mal. No fucking way was I prepared to let anything happen to you. I thought it would be best for everyone if you hated me. It's proved fucking good so far, hasn't it?" I can't help the sarcasm that rolls off my tongue. I finally allow my twitching hand to reach out and cup her angelic face. "I don't want you to leave Jess, but this is the only way I can be sure that I can't hurt you again."

Jess

My heads thoroughly mashed. I mean seriously, what the fuck just happened? I sit in front of Melissa, completely flabbergasted and I know that Max is still waiting for me in the car. After that head-fuck of a conversation that we just had, he made it pretty clear that he will be the one taking me back to work. Part of me should be happy right now, knowing that Stella isn't in the picture. Yes, the bitch is still going to be a massive problem but still, knowing she isn't keeping Max warm at night calms me somewhat. A major improvement is that Max has just opened up to me in more ways than I ever thought imaginable and I'm completely at a loss for words. I have a hell of a lot of questions, that's for sure, but for now I think I'll settle for a bloody large strong drink.

"About flipping time girly. What was the hold up?"

"I've just had it confirmed that your brother is an absolute head-fuck."

"Oh, so you guys talked it out, then?" Her eyes shine bright, flickering with hope as she waits for my reply.

"More like he did the talking and I just sat there and listened. Oh, is that one for me?" I ask eying the delicious looking cocktail that she places before me. I subtlety try to change the subject, but Liss is having none of it, fuck my life right now.

"You betcha. Drink up and spill it. Did he finally explain what's going on in that crazy little head of his? What went down with Stella? Please tell me he explained that little predicament to you?"

"Jeez, catch a breath." I toy with the straw and stir my mojito around slowly before I respond to her onslaught of questions. It still feels weird discussing this with Liss. "Yeah, I brought it up. I don't think he would have openly started to discuss it if I hadn't brought it up to begin with, if I'm being honest. I'm still not one hundred percent convinced though. Do they have a history?"

"Who Max and Stella? Are you shitting me? Max never, ever mixes business with pleasure. He's too career driven to do something like that. Well until you anyway."

"Oh, here we go again." I think to myself.

"Hey, if my brother has opened up to you, then I'm pretty shocked. Max doesn't explain himself to anyone; he's never needed to before. You, my girly, have obviously affected him in more ways than anyone has realised."

"Maybe." Possible hope is flying around in my head that this could have been a misunderstanding after all. "Apparently she picked up on the wrong signals or something."

"What a bitch. I just knew she would try something like this one day, and I've warned Max from the start. I don't like her at all. She's like a fucking leech around him. Does he know you're staying?"

"No. It didn't cross my mind to tell him. It's pointless anyway seeing as though he feels it's for the best, so that he can't hurt me."

"Absolute bollocks. Ignore that foreign language that men speak. What you need to do, is decide what happens now?"

"I have no idea, why don't you ask him? He's sat waiting in the car to take me back once we're done." I watch in silence as she takes her phone out of her bag and makes a call.

"Max, do me a favour and fuck off. I'll bring her back once we're done. She doesn't need a fucking babysitter." I'm not sure if he says anything back to her, or if he even has the chance to do so, as she hangs up pretty fast. "Sorted, now let's get some food."

Lunch goes by pretty fast and before I know it, butterflies begin to form in my stomach just knowing that Max will be waiting for me back at the office.

"I guess I won't be seeing you at home tonight, then?" The devilish grin that dances on Melissa's face tells me what she thinks I'll be getting up to. She couldn't be any further away from the truth. No way am I just going to go and jump straight back into bed with him. My body aches at the thought, but I need to be strong. This time, I'll be the one calling the shots. Or at least I'll try my goddamn best to.

"Why, where else would I be? Are you kicking me out so soon?" I playfully tease her.

"Not at all, I just thought that maybe you and Max had some making up to do?"

"I don't think so Liss. Wait... Do you and Heath have plans for tonight?" Maybe I am overstaying my welcome. By the sounds of things, these two are walking on egg shells as it is, and I'd hate to intrude. "I don't want to get in the way of your alone time."

"Oh shit. I forgot to call him. No, no, not at all. I just wasn't sure if you were going to abandon me for that stubborn arse brother of mine."

"That isn't going to happen, Liss. I'm pretty happy staying with you. As long as it's still okay, of course?" Melissa breaks out into a fit of giggles, why I'm not so sure."What's so funny?"

"You know that Max isn't going to be okay with that, don't you? Be prepared for him to make a stand when it comes to where you stay, Jess."

"Are you being serious? There's no bloody way he's going to be telling me where I can and can't stay."

"Hey, I'm just trying to give you a heads up here. He's completely smitten with you. Come on Jess, does Max look like the type of guy who is going to share you, *with anyone*?"

I'm surprised to see that Max isn't lurking on the pavement waiting for me like he'd promised. Clearly he does listen to someone. I make a mental note to keep that in mind the next time I need to make him listen, all I need to do is call Liss. When I get back to the office Max isn't anywhere to be seen. Our floor, as usual is empty. I try to feel unaffected by his absence, but a part of me actually couldn't wait to see him and pick up where we left off, earlier. I'm a glutton for bloody punishment.

Dragging my defeated body towards my office I can't help but feel disappointed that he wasn't here waiting for me. *Shitting hell, Jess. You told yourself you weren't going to make this easy for him and less than a day of him being back in your life, you're dropping all those walls.*

I switch on my monitor as soon as I'm at my desk. Getting my head stuck into work has worked out okay for me in the past, but somehow I know this time it's going to be completely different. Max isn't Josh. He's stubborn as hell, but that's what makes him so, *him*. Max Wild isn't someone you can just forget about. I only wish he was. It would make my life so much easier. Looking down at my keyboard, I see a post-it note on the keys.

Meet me in the spa. I'll be waiting... Max.

Meet him in the spa? Why would he be in the spa?

Doesn't he know that we have work to do? I'm really beginning to question his work ethic. I'm not going to go rushing down there, no matter how curious I am. While I wait for some time to pass, god it's agonising making myself wait, but I will hold it out. I'm not going to let him think that all he needs to do is click his fingers and I'll come running. I decide to check in on Mal. Daisy answers on the third ring and I can hear the football booming in the background.

"Oh Jess dear, we were just about to call you actually." She sings down the line.

"You were? I thought I'd call to see how the patient is getting on and to see if you needed anything when I finish up work?"

"Oh I wouldn't worry about him dear. He's perfectly fine. He's resting in front of the television as we speak. Anyway, while I have you, we're having a little get together on Friday night. It's more of an official welcome home party for Mal. We'd both love it if you could make it."

"Of course I'll be there. You know I wouldn't miss it for the world. Just let me know the time, oh wait, you'll also need to give me the address, too." I say as I remember that I haven't been to their new home yet.

"Well Melissa's coming too dear, so she will be able to bring you and it's from 7pm onwards."

"Brilliant. I can't wait to see you both properly and I must say Daisy, I'm a little bit excited to explore your new humble abode."

"It's absolutely perfect. I'll warn you, you might not want to leave once you've been." That's probably true. Daisy knows that I'm a sucker for a good property.

Deciding that I have made Max wait long enough, I nip to the ladies to freshen up and to check that I look presentable. I feel like a kid again when I was asked out on my first date. Why do I feel so nervous around him? Why can't I do the right thing and stay away from him? He's obviously got a pretty good reason for wanting me to go back home, but yet he takes time out of his day to come and see me. Ugh major head fuck.

I see him as soon as I enter the spa. His bright blue eyes glisten from the reflection of the water. His five o'clock shadow makes him look even more ruggedly beautiful than usual. Seriously there are no words that do Max justice, when it comes to describing how beautiful he actually is. I still have no idea why I have been called down here, but I slowly step towards him in the hope of finding out.

"What took you so long?" His voice echoes off the walls and his face is serious, his brows coming together as he silently brews over whatever he's thinking in that sexy mind of his.

"In case you forgot, I actually have work to do while I'm here."

"That can wait. As of now, you can take a break and relax here with me instead."

"I'd much rather finish what I have started." As inviting as it sounds, I'm here to work and I need to remember that.

"You and me both angel." He leans over and reaches for my arm and pulls me close to him. "I've missed you and that smart mouth too goddamn much."

"I'm not sure about this, Max." Hesitantly I pull back to look at him. I told myself I wouldn't be a push over again and I'm going to stand true to my word. One thing keeps filtering to the forefront of my mind though, no matter how much I try to push it back. It's not that he shut me out, I completely understand his reasons for that, even if I don't agree with them. No, the one thing that keeps pulling me back, is Stella. I know he has explained what happened, but to me that doesn't make me feel much better. She's a fucking problem and I think she always will be.

"Aren't I supposed to have a P.A? I'm sure that's what you said? If I had one of those, then I would have someone to arrange my work."

"I believe I did Miss Townsend, but your P.A seems to be a little work shy, so I'll need to talk her into it again or find you a replacement."

"Oh that sounds good, you could get a replacement too and we could share that one." The words are out of my mouth before I can stop them. I can't believe I have just asked him to fire Stella. Oh well, it's what the bitch deserves and it would be pretty fucking amazing to see the smug look being wiped from her face. "What do you say? It's an amazing idea."

"She's harmless, Jess."

"Harmless? Come on. You can't actually believe that? She's been dying to get her claws into you for ages, if not longer, if what I'm told is true."

"Oh Jess, I already explained all of this to you earlier. I can't, and won't fire her. Understood?" His tone takes on a stern edge and I know I'm beginning to push him too far.

"Well maybe you're explaining this to the wrong person, Max. As far as she was concerned this morning, she has already claimed what is *rightfully* hers. It also didn't skip her attention that I was heading back home, and that obviously couldn't happen soon enough according to her. So tell me, do you expect me to work with that psycho?"

"I'll have a word with her. She has a tendency to see how far she can push someone. Wait… did you just say was? Does that mean you're staying?"

"Until my work here is finished, yes. I'm not a quitter Max. No matter what life throws at me, if I'm in the middle of a project, I'll make sure I finish it." He puts his hand around my neck and pulls me into him and this time, I don't resist. He's far from forgiven, but I think he's worth another chance.

"How about you let me be your project?" He smiles and then his lips are on mine again, searching with a hunger and need so powerful, that I have no choice but to comply.

"I thought if I stayed you would only end up hurting me?"

"I said the people I let in always end up getting hurt because of me, angel. I would never, ever hurt you intentionally." I allow him to tilt my head back as his lips seek out mine. Max Wild is doing it to me again, and this time I think I'll flow with it, but keep my eyes peels for any signs of him slipping again.

We spend the rest of the afternoon in spa, completely alone with the facilities closed off to all of the other guests. All I have wanted to do is touch him, feel him against me again like I used too but surprisingly, I remained strong, only allowing him to kiss me. Who knew this girl could have so much willpower? It's been nice to actually spend some time together with it being just the two of us, with no one else around. After the events of the past two weeks I think it's what we both needed. Some downtime without any expectations is definitely a must.

"What are you doing later?" His rustic tone brings me back to the present as we leave the hotel. My hair is still slightly damp and goose bumps prickle my skin from the cold evening air.

"I'm not sure, probably gossiping about life's little dramas over a bottle of wine."

"Why don't you come back to mine, I'll cook us something nice and we could watch a movie, or something."

"Melissa would eat me alive if I ditched her for you, but I guess you knew that already." Judging by the innocent smile that graces his face, yes he does.

"Jeez, she's really enjoying having you around' hey?"

"Can you blame her? It can't have been easy growing up being surrounded by guys, she needs a girl to vent to every once in a while, we have these little things called hormones and they can be nasty little shits if we don't let them out. Plus she's a great girl and I enjoy spending time with her. In a way, she feels like my Jen away from home. It's comforting, yet scary how similar they are."

"And an utterly lethal combination for men."

"I can't believe you didn't go home with Max. Oh girly, he's definitely bitten off more than he can chew with you, hasn't he? It's going to be amazing to watch. So, how was this afternoon?" I know what she's doing, the sneaky Cow. She's digging for dirt and as much as I like to think of her as a friend, there is no way that I'm discussing personal relations between me and Max with her. No way. I decide to keep it short and sweet instead. "It was pretty productive, I guess."

"Seriously." She slams the palm of her hand down on the table in feigned anger. "That's all you're going to give me. You're one tight arse bitch, Jess Townsend. Do you know that?"

"What do you want to know? I was at work, there's nothing interesting to tell. You on the other hand are a different ball game. What were *you* doing? Actually what do you do during the day, anyway?" I've never once seen her work since I've been here. I've never really felt the need to ask, but since she's making a habit of prying into my daily life, I think it's only fair.

"Me? As if you don't know already. I just walk around

looking beautiful all day, honey. Oh and I like to shop sometimes too."

"Really? Do you not get bored? Maybe you should get out and socialise some more. Who knows you might even enjoy it."

"That came out completely wrong. I thought you Brits were supposed to love sarcasm? I have a job, I just can't be arsed with it right now, so I decided to take a hiatus."

"Fair enough." What else can I say to that? She obviously doesn't have the financial worry that most people have and if she's happy, then fair play to her.

"Heath's stopping by later. I hope you don't mind?"

"Will you stop that? Seriously, it's your house, not mine. Who you have come around, is completely up to you."

"Jess, while you're here, it's just as much your home too. Make sure you don't ever forget that."

Max

I look around before I exit the car and try to collect myself. It's been years since I've been here, and I would have bet my fucking life that I would never have to cross those fucking doors again. Yet here I am, scared shitless once more and completely out of my comfort zone. I never have control when I'm here. It's zapped from me the minute I enter, to the minute I leave and I fucking hate it with a passion. I need to do this. I need to do it for me, for Jess. Fuck I need to do this for *us.*

If we're ever going to have any slither of hope at giving this a go, I really need to get some control over my life again. I need to close off those demons once and for all, regardless of how much of a dent it makes in my pride. I swallow and take a few deep breaths to prepare myself. What I wouldn't give right now to turn back around and forget I ever fucking came here.

As I enter the main doors I'm greeted by a familiar, yet unwelcome sight. Nothing seems to have changed. Nothing, even the plant pots look like they haven't been touched over the years. The decor, the smell, shit. Even the clichéd posters remain firmly in place on the walls. Images of the past begin to swirl in my mind and I try to fight the nausea that follows.

"Good to see you again, Mr Wild." The receptionist looks up and greets me. I take in the girl before me, polite and a smile that spreads ear to ear.

"Sasha." I nod. I haven't seen her in years and to be honest I thought she'd left town a few years back. Life's full of little surprises.

"Doctor Hutchins will be with you soon. Is there anything I can get you while you're waiting?" Her fingers twirl within her hair as she asks me this, a shy yet knowing look dances across her face. No, not this time I want to say, but instead I just shake my head and make my way over to the waiting area. Today is a major head fuck. How many more hurdles are going to be thrown at me before it ends?

It feels like I've been sat twiddling my thumbs for hours, when I finally hear my name being called.

"Max, please come on through." Don hasn't changed one bit. The old dog's still looking as youthful and presentable as ever. It's a mighty shame that after all this time, I have to see him again on these terms. It's not much of a surprise at this stage to see that his office is also still the same as it was the last time I was here. The walls are all neutral while the furniture remains black. His desk spans the right hand side, while a thick plush leather sofa spans the left.

"So what brings you back here, Max?" His tone remains light, yet his curious face tells me he knows this isn't for a regular drop in session. My hands begin to shake involuntarily as I try to figure out what I'm going to say. I fix my gaze on the window in front of me, while trying to delay my answer. How the hell am I supposed to start a conversation that I never thought I'd have to repeat again?

"Seriously Don, you really need to ask?" I snap and then my shoulders slump as my body admits defeat. I'm here, being judged once again when all I want to do is get the hell out of here. *Awesome fucking plan Wild.*

"Well, it's been quite some time Max. Why don't you take a seat?"

"I don't fucking want a seat. I shouldn't even be here for god sake. All I want is for this nightmare to fuck off and never come back." I point to my temple as the rage burns within me. Normally I'm good at keeping it in, but here in this office? Not a fucking chance.

"Let's start from the beginning then, and we'll see where we go from there." It pisses me off that no matter how much I vent at him, he still remains as calm and collected as ever. I guess the sooner I get this over with, the better.

I sit down on the sofa and I can feel his eyes burning into the inner depths of my blackened soul. My body is all rigid from the built up tension, my jaw working overtime and I try to regulate my breathing by inhaling some sharp deep breaths.

"How are you feeling at the moment?"

"Seriously? Like a fucking knob, Don. You know I don't want to be here, so let's get on with it, hey?" As soon as I'm done here I'll be hitting the surf. Why have I fucking come here anyway?

"Angry, frustrated? I can't help you, if you're not prepared to help me Max. How about a trigger? Is there anything that could have happened to set these feelings off again?"

"Heaps of shit that I've let build up over time. The past few weeks have been one hell of a roller coaster to say the least." I knew my decision to go back to England was reckless, but I thought I could control everything now. Don remains seated in his chair, analysing me while making notes in his file. "I went home." I say on a defeated sigh. His head snaps up at my words.

"Home?" He says curiously, all note taking suddenly forgotten for a moment.

"Yes, home. Well, the one true place that I first called home, anyway. Mal, you remember my uncle Mal? Well he runs a property business back in England and I've been asking him to come over here for years to work with me."

"I see. The creativity obviously flows through the genes. So what happened when you were there? Is this when the memories and feelings returned?"

"Oh, some fucking feelings were present alright, but nothing that I couldn't handle."

"Go on..."

"I'd rather pass on that Don." There is no way that I am bringing Jess into this if I can help it. No one else needs to know what happens with us, but *us.*

"You know the steps Max. Start at the beginning and work your way up."

"Do you know what? Fuck this. Talking about it isn't going to do shit. I knew it was a bad idea, but I needed to try it."

I get up and storm out of the room without a backwards glance and almost knock Sasha out in the process, as the fire door slams against the wall.

"Hey Max, wait." I hear her call after me. I stop and turn to see her sauntering towards me. She's still as beautiful and breath-taking as I remember, but on closer inspection she seems to have lost her spark somewhat along the way. "I never expected to see you back here that's for sure."

"That would make the both of us, then. What's with you? I never had you down as they type to stick around here for long either?"

"What can I say?" She laughs. "I guess the place must have grown on me after all. Plus, Don's a good guy." She looks up at me from under her eyelashes, displaying that come to bed with me look, that I know only too well. A few months ago I probably would have played along with her, a nice, good easy distraction to take my mind away from the constant bullshit that's suddenly occupying it. But now? Now I have to get my shit together and sort my fucking head out. I need to prove to myself and to Jess, that I can be the man that she deserves.

"Well it's been good seeing you, Sash. I hate to do this, but I've gotta shoot. Tell Don I'll rearrange some other time when my heads not so jumbled." I feel her hand rest on my arm just as I turn to leave for the second time.

"Maybe we could grab a coffee, talk about it?"

"Maybe some other time? Now's really not a good time to be dragging up shit from the past." I really should have seen this one coming.

"Okay. That's fine, I get it. How about you call me when you feel up to it?" I nod in her direction, anything to get out of here in one piece, yet I know that I have no intention to call her, whatsoever. Call me a cold hearted bastard all you want, but it is what it is. I've found my angel and she's all that I want. If I can't have her, then I don't want anyone else as no one could come close to her, not in a million fucking years.

My lungs welcome the fresh air as if I have been starved of it and my head slowly begins to feel a little relief from the pressure that was there a few moments ago. Maybe I shouldn't have returned to Australia. Maybe I should have stayed with Luke and started all over again. If I have learnt anything over the last few weeks, then it's that England is *home*. England is where I feel like the true Max. The guy that I have always wanted to be, but the mother fucking demons inside of me have prevented him from shining through. Maybe I have made a massive fucking mistake in coming back here? Maybe coming back has opened the can of worms that I don't seem to be able to get rid of.

Jess

"Green or orange? Oh, maybe this red one would be better?"

"How about you close your eyes and pick one at random?" I suggest to the very indecisive Melissa sat opposite me. She's been bloody sat here deciding what polish she should choose for the past hour. How bloody hard can it be?

"But the blue's really pretty, too."

"For fucks sake Liss, just choose one." I laugh at her as she pulls a sour face at me. I know she has missed out on having female company for a few years, but this is taking the piss. "Here, this one will suit your complexion." I pass her the purple one and a mega-watt smile spreads across her face. I could get used to having a salon and spa in the workplace. I arrived at the office to find that Melissa had already booked us in for a full afternoon pamper session. Bless her heart, she'd even rescheduled all of today's meetings too. Apparently she was very much entitled to do so, and according to her, Max would agree; so who was I to argue?

"Personally, I'm just getting a mani and pedi, that right there makes me a happy girl. Please tell me you've decided what you're going to wear?" I dread the answer that is about to come from her mouth. I retract my previous statements. This girl isn't like Jen at all, she's bloody worse.

"No. Have you?"

"Erm, I kind of hopped on a plane without much

variety. I should be here working not going out to parties."

"Oh shut up moaning. Let your hair down for once. Plus it's your boss' party anyway."

"Maybe my lovely housemate could kindly loan me the use of her wardrobe?" I say while fluttering my eyelashes and flashing her my most innocent smile.

"Only," She points her finger at me, "If I get to choose."

I agree, not sure if I'm going to live to regret this. But I need something to wear and fast.

"Don't look so horrified, Jess. You'll look fucking hot and you know it."

We spend most of the afternoon lounging around in the spa. It's becoming quite the habit and I may need to watch I don't get addicted to this place, yet right now I have no intention whatsoever of moving anytime soon. At least not until I hear the high pitched cackle of the she-demon.

"Oh well. Don't we look cosy, down here doing nothing?" Her tone is laced with sarcasm and has my back up instantly. I wish she would just piss off once and for all. Before I get my say, Melissa pipes up.

"What do you want, Stella? Not even all the cosmetics in here are going to do you any favours love." The ice in Melissa's eyes is clear to see, and I'm glad I'm not the only one who sees her for what she really is.

"I would like to know why my staff are down here having a jolly good time, while I'm busy picking up the pieces."

"Your staff? Don't make me laugh. Did Max hand all of this over to you too, when your imaginary relationship started? What's up Stella? Do you not think that me and my brother *talk*? Oh, and a little FYI, you're the one who clearly isn't doing your job as the amazing glorified secretary that you are, because if you were, then you would have noticed that there is nothing in the diary today."

I watch as Stella's eyes narrow, as Melissa sing songs all of this too her. Finally her eyes land on me, pure cold anger is staring back at me. Well that feeling is mutual.

"I told Max not to hire you."

"Excuse me?" I finally say after the shock of her hurling that at me, slowly sinks in. "Who Max employs is none of your business." I reply but she ignores me as if I haven't spoken.

"Melissa, you're shocking at what you do. The only reason why you are here now, is because you're Max's little sister and he feels sorry for you. Yes me and your brother also talk too you know."

" And why are you here, exactly?" My chest aches at the pain that is suddenly in Melissa's voice at Stella's words. I don't believe any of it. Not for a bloody second. Anyone can see how much Melissa means to Max and he's not the type of person to have someone hanging around just because he feels sorry for them. Family or not.

"Because Max needs me. He always has and he always will."

"Fuck off Stella. You're one delusional cow. How does he need you? He's never needed anyone in his life. Well, until *she* walked into his life, anyway." Melissa points her finger in my direction and Stella looks at me as if really seeing me for the very first time and she remains deadly silent.

"Oops... Did your loveable Max not tell you that he and Jess have sorted everything out now, No? Well that's a mighty shame. I guess you won't be able to play your bullshit little games with people's lives anymore will you? Maybe next time you need to try a little bit harder, Stella."

"You would do well to remember who you are speaking to Melissa, especially when you start to hurl out allegations."

"Oh piss off. Why are you still here? Max is never going to want you so deal with it, instead of hanging around like a desperate fucking woman that can't get laid. It's embarrassing."

I just sit here and watch them bouncing off each other and it takes everything I have to remain seated. If I thought Stella was a bitch before, then today has only confirmed it. I really didn't think it was possible for someone to dislike Stella as much as me, but Melissa is doing a pretty good job. Needless to say, it's not long before Stella turns on her designer clad heels and storms off to only god knows where.

I decide to head back up to the office before we leave, just to see if I have any important emails that need singing off for the day. After my pamper day, all I want to do is sleep, but I know that Liss will never let that happen. Just as I exit the lift I see that beautiful face looking back at me. The pure image of him all suited and booted causes shivers of excitement to course through my body, and my heart begins to race. I stop dead in my tracks, which in turn causes Melissa to crash into the back of me.

"Seriously guys, can you stop fucking each other with your eyes for a few minutes. It's sickly." I feel my face heat over at her words, but the chemistry that is still between us is evident. He stands facing me, Melissa's words having no effect on him whatsoever. His eyes search mine and I have to fight to stop my hands from reaching out to touch his ruffled hair. Desire pours from him and he doesn't even try to hide it. Shitting hell, this man is bad for my health.

Melissa clears her throat to try and break the connection between us and I just about make out her words. "Guys come on; this really isn't cool for me to see, you know."

"So you finally decided to pull your lazy arse into work then?" Max says. At first I think he's talking to me, but then his eyes reach Melissa's and I can't help but feel confused. To be honest it doesn't take all that much these days, it's like a regular occurrence.

"I thought I'd get out of the house for a bit, you know stretch my legs and all that?"

"What do you mean?" Both heads turn in unison to look at me.

"After all this time you and still haven't told her, hey?" A huge mischievous grin dances across Max's face. Obviously he feels like he now has something over Melissa and now I am curious to know what that is. "Melissa here is your, or should I say was, your unruly personal assistant. Not that she's assisted you much on the work front anyway."

"Seriously?" I look to Melissa to gage some kind of reaction from her. How could she have kept this from me? I don't mind doing the work that I have done so far, I'm used to going solo and I love it that way, but I guess it would have been nice for her to tell me if she didn't want to do it. "Why haven't you told me?"

"Hey... I wasn't sure if I wanted to do it in the first place. Come on, would you work with that fucking dragon full time? It was a nightmare while Max was away." Well she has a pretty valid point on that front, but I'd be lying if I said I didn't feel hurt that she kept this from me.

"I expect you to be here on Monday, Liss. The time that you have had off already, can be classed as a holiday." I say to her and Max chuckles beside me. My heart swells a little at this, knowing that he approves of my ways. He really is something else.

"You're going to be a fucking nightmare to work for, aren't you?" She asks which makes Max laugh even more

"No, not at all." I smile back at her and right in this moment, I know that she's going to bloody hate me.

After raiding Melissa's wardrobe for the evening, I decide to settle in some simple, yet sexy black skinny jeans. I'm immensely thankful that my arse just about squeezes into them without an overhang. I team them with baby blue patent heels and a floaty blue top which shows off my curves in all the right places. After toying with my hair for the past half an hour, I decide to leave it down and straighten it for a change in the hope that I give off the casual look. My make-up is kept simple with nudes, but I add my fail proof red lipstick which never fails to draw attention to my already generously sized lips.

I'm excited to see Mal and Daisy in their new home but I'm nervous as hell about bumping into Max. I know the whole Stella situation has been dealt with, but something about me getting close to him again causes me to panic. I just hope that as soon as I've got a drink in me I'll start to calm down.

"Fucking hell Jess. Are you trying to put my brother in hospital? I think we've had enough heart attacks in this family already girly, don't you?"

"Shit, is it too much? I was aiming for casual." I say as I wander into the living room.

"Nothing about *you* could ever be causal. You look hot as hell." Suddenly I feel very self-conscious and begin tugging at the hem of my top. "You look fucking amazing, quit messing, okay?" She pulls my hand away from my top and gives me a stern look. A look that scarily has Max written all over it.

"Is Heath going to be there?" I ask trying to change the subject.

"You bet he is. He'll most likely be with Max all night, so I'll have to admire him from afar. Plus, neither of us want to raise any suspicions."

"Do you really think he'll care that much if you tell him? Maybe he'd be more pissed with the fact that you kept it from him."

"I'm not even going to give that a fucking response." She snaps back at me.

They've got to be overreacting. Yes I get the whole protective big brother scenario, but this is going a little too far, even for a control freak like Max. From what I have learnt so far, it seems that all Max has wanted is for someone to look after her and who better than his pal?

While Liss finishes off touching up, I draw out my phone from my clutch and type out a quick message.

I miss you like crazy. X

"Ready?"
"As I'll ever be."

Max

This house still feels fucking empty. I spent years designing the perfect home where I'd feel comfortable, and what for? What used to feel like my perfect getaway, now feels void of anything. It's like a show home. It looks fucking good, *really fucking good,* but what use is that to me, if I don't enjoy being here anymore? The place feels bare. It's far too quiet, something that I used to thrive on after a busy day and dare I say it, now it all feels fucking pointless. I have all this space with nothing but me to fill it. Space also used to me my thing, but now my head's getting more and more fucked up the more time I spend here alone.

I need to find a way to get Jess to come back to where she belongs. *With me.* I don't like knowing that she is more comfortable with Liss, than she is here with me. Fuck my life and what it's become.

Setting my Cadillac into park, I look out at Mal's new house. He sure seems happy here and that in itself makes me happy. It's all I've ever wanted to do. To try and repay him in some way for everything that they have done for me and Liss over the years. They have both been there for us, no matter what and to see them happy gives me a sense of pride that maybe, just maybe, I have done something worthwhile in this life.

Tonight, I really need to talk to Jess. I need to know what's happening with us, and if she feels like it's worth giving it another shot. I know that I have fucked up so far, royally fucked up, but the Stella issue was purely

bad timing of a fucked up situation and I've explained
that to Jess already. I just hope that it's enough.

Jess

"Oh what do you know? My so called daughter finally answers her goddamn phone to mummy dearest." My mother's voice echoes down the line and I can tell she is drunk from the slurring of her words.

"Hi mum. What's up?" I say sharply. I can't help the snap in my tone even though I try my best to hide my irritation. Holding my finger up, I signal to Melissa that I'll only be a minute.

"I don't see you anymore Jessica. Why don't you bother to call me? You're supposed to be my daughter, or are am I not good enough for your fancy little life anymore?" Oh god. Here we go. As soon as alcohol touches her lips the world and everyone in it, is suddenly against her.

"You know why I don't call you anymore, mum. You made it pretty clear last time we spoke that you wanted nothing to do with me. I believe your exact words were that you wished me dead." At my words, Melissa's head whips around to face me, causing her unruly curls to bounce a few times. I just shrug at her to try and remove the outrageous look she has on her face.

"What is it with you? Every fucking thing always has to be about you doesn't it? You're just like your father, you know? Only out for yourself in this world and you don't care who you hurt in the process."

"Well it's been lovely taking to you mum, as always. I've got to go." I desperately want to get her off this phone. Normally I'd be okay to deal with it, but I know that Melissa is stood before me and all I want to do is cry. My hands begin to shake as I press the end call button on my phone and I bite my bottom lip to prevent the tears that threaten to fall. After everything, she still has the audacity to blame me because dad walked out on us. I understand that she's still hurting, I completely get it, but jeez, she's never tried to let go. Instead hate and anger have been bubbling away inside her ever since and all she can do is spit her poison. Not to mention that my mother can hold a grudge for a bloody long time. I wouldn't mind, but I haven't spoken to her for months, so why is she suddenly calling now after all this time?

"What the fuck was that about? Was that your mum?" Melissa is on me in an instant, her hand rubbing frantically on my shoulder in circular motions trying to calm the shaking that is taking over my entire body.

"It's nothing new. I'm used to it, honestly. I guess it's just the shock of her calling after so long."

"Still, that's not right Jess. No mother should ever speak to their child like that. *Ever.*" No they shouldn't. I know that, but it's something that I have had to get used to over the years.

"Honestly, I'd rather just forget about it. Now." I say straightening in my top and painting on my big girl face. "Are we ready to go?"

"You bet'cha."

I'm still livid at my mum's out of the blue outburst, when we pull up outside Mal and Daisy's. I'm still rocking my big girl panties, but deep down every single hurtful word slices me open inside. I often wonder what she would have been like if things had've worked out differently and if my dad had stayed around. Maybe she has always been that way deep down, and I hate to think that maybe that's one of the reasons that he walked out on us. I've never tried to contact him to find out the reasons behind his actions. He's never tried to contact me and I've never really felt the urge to contact him, either. He didn't just turn his back and walk out on my mum; he did it to *me* too. I feel a soft hand rest on my shoulder which makes me jump and pulls me away from my thoughts.

"What do you say, you ready to face the world, or do you need some more time?" My hands clasp together in my lap as mixed emotions run wild within me. Why, oh why does she get to me like this. It's ridiculous. Nothing she says to me should bother me anymore. I take a deep breath and gather my thoughts, before plastering on the biggest smile I can muster.

"Let's do this."

We're greeted by Daisy at the door. She looks a pure picture of health and contentment in her new home, and I really don't blame her. It's modern yet classic all at the same time. Absolutely beautiful. Both myself and Melissa are taken through to the kitchen area where people seem to be gathering. It's large, very open spaced and has more knobs and gadgets than I ever thought possible.

I sense him before I see him. His presence is electric. His back is currently facing me, but I'd recognise that strong set of shoulders anywhere. His posture is quite casual as he stands with his legs shoulder width apart next to Heath. Even dressed in jeans and a plain black shirt, with his sleeves pushed up to his elbows causes excitement to ripple through my body. I look down at my outfit and feel slightly overkill. As if automatically sensing that I have arrived, he turns on his heels to take me in. With one hand in his pocket and the other holding a beer to his mouth, he really is the picture of utter perfection. Those piercing blue eyes penetrate into my soul as he undresses me bit by bit. No matter how much time passes, no matter how much I etch his beautiful face into my memory, it always feels like I am seeing him again for the very first time. I notice his eyes grow darker, from the alcohol? I'm not too sure, but they teasingly roam seductively up and down my body, resting at each of my curves, until he slowly raises them back up to meet mine once again.

"Come on through, dear. There's no need for you to just stand there." Daisy says as she waves me over. I force myself to tear my gaze away from Max so I don't appear rude to our host. Standing there in her outfit, she looks the perfect picture of summer and health, which is quite apt for the party after all.

"Where's the man of this party, then? Don't tell me that he's sat watching the bloody football again?"

"Of course he's watching the football. Jess, I'd be worried if he wasn't. Oh Melissa darling you look beautiful as always."

Melissa flashes a knowing smile to Daisy before throwing her glossy black hair over her shoulder as she spots Heath heading towards us.

"Thank you, Daisy." She says, while leaning in to give her a swift peck on the cheek.

"Come on now girls. Why don't we head outside and I'll get us all a drink."

The house is beautiful and from what I can tell, I'd say both Daisy and Mal seem to have settled in rather well. Everything is on one floor, which is convenient for Mal, but god it's spacious. Where Max's house is modern and bright, Mal and Daisy's house is much more homely. Family photographs now hang in frames along the walls and you can tell Daisy has been busy adding a woman's touch to the place.

"Wow, Daisy this really is something else." I say

unable to hold back.

"Isn't it just. Max knew just how we like things and has it all arranged. He's a good man, Jess. Don't be fooled by his *Mr arrogant* persona." She pats me on the arm as she says this. To comfort me, maybe? "I know he can be immensely difficult at times, but his heart is always in the right place. All he needs is someone to remind him how to use it."

I literally have no words to reply to her, none whatsoever. My guess is that he has been pretty destroyed over something in the past. The question is *what*? I'd like to think he'll eventually tell me when he's ready and if not, then that's fine by me.

"Come on girl, let's move." I look to my secret keeper stood before me bouncing from one foot to the other. Can I actually bring myself to ask her such personal questions about her brother? I've never, ever been the snooping type before, so why should I start now?

"What a lovely home Mal."

"Flower, its bloody good to see you. How's things going with the development?" Seriously is he asking about work at *his* welcome home party? Of course he is.

"Everything's under control and not for you to be worrying yourself with." The hairs on the back of my neck stand up and goose bumps break out over my arms at the powerful, deep voice that sounds behind me.

"Jess." The way he says my name, has my knees going weak. Every fucking time. In seconds he stands next to me and I quickly grab my drink from Melissa and toss it back. I look at her with a pleading stare for her to help me, maybe pass me another drink, but all the sneaky cow does is smile and walks off in the opposite direction; towards Heath. *The bitch.*

"Max." I nod towards him and a sexy curve forms on

his lips as he takes in my discomfort in front of Mal and Daisy. Why does he do this? It's pure fucking torture. Torture that's somewhat increased, when he places the palm of his hand against the base of my spine causing a mass of delicious tingles to travel south.

"I've missed you angel." His words kiss my ear as he leans is close to whisper them to me. He's not even bothered that Mal and Daisy are in the same room as us. "You look fucking beautiful."

"You don't scrub up so bad yourself." I laugh. Suddenly feeling much more relaxed around everyone, I look up into his eyes and give him a shy smile. One that says *"yes I do want you, more than you will ever know."*

Max

I feel like I've gone back in time. It feels so fucking surreal. Here I stand, Mal, Liss and Daisy all around me doing normal family stuff. It feels just like it used to do, except now instead of reliving my memories in black and white, they now have a glow to them and they start to shine so fucking bright like never before.

Jess.

What a fucking woman. No matter what, she always finds ways to surprise me, no end. Even if she doesn't know that she is doing it. Unable to stop myself, I make my way back over to where she stands, the pull far too strong to resist. As soon as I am close to her, a feeling of contentment surrounds me. It still feels crazy as hell, but I like it. Wild thoughts begin to take over my mind. All the things we could do together, the possibilities could be endless, if only I could get my fucking act together. I've felt what it's like to be without her, and there is no fucking way that I'm prepared to go through that hell again.

I nod my head in acknowledgement towards Mal and Daisy and then step closer to Jess.

"Allow me to take you on a guided tour, Miss Townsend?" I ask, as I rest my hand at the base of her spine so my fingers lightly touch her. Tonight she will be coming home with me, that I am fucking sure off. It's been far too long and her reaction towards my touch tells me that she feels exactly the same.

"Thank you but I'm okay. Hasn't anyone ever told you that it's rude to go snooping around other people's homes?"

"To Mal and Daisy, you're family Jess, so they won't mind at all. Come on, I'd love to show you around."

"Still, I'd rather not." She licks her bottom lip and I want nothing more than to capture that delicate tongue with my own. She smiles at me, fully aware of what she is doing to me, as she smooth's down her blouse. She's lucky I have respect for the people that are around me, otherwise that top, fuck everything she has on would be gracing the floor right now.

"Okay everyone. The barbecue's ready." Mal shouts at the top of his lungs. A gruntled and frustrated sigh escapes me and I don't miss the chuckle that leaves Jess's mouth. Someone is clearly enjoying themselves. Shit, what do I care? It's fucking amazing to see that smile again.

No sooner are we all gathered together outside on the patio, Mal stands and chimes his fork against the glass.

"Well, I'm not the best with words as you all know, but I'd like to try and raise a toast." Laughter filled with happiness erupts around us and my chest fills with pride for this man stood before me. "Firstly I'd like to personally thank you all. For being here tonight, but also more importantly for taking time out of your busy day to day lives to rally around me and my distraught, darling wife here. As much as she would love the life insurance pay out, she's going to have to wait a while longer for those endless shopping trips."

Only Mal could stand there and make a joke about his health. He's always been the one to make light of a heavy situation.

"Here, here." Daisy shouts through an emotional filled voice.

"Well, with that said, I just want you to know how

thankful I am to each and every one of you for being here tonight and for your prayers and support. I don't think there will ever be enough words to tell you how much that means to me. Now woman, where's that food." He demands as he takes a seat in his rightful place, at the head of the table. If I turn out to be half the man that Mal is, I'll be one happy fucking guy

Jess

I've had an anxious niggling feeling in the pit of my stomach all night. I'm not sure if it's down to seeing Max, or the unexpected call from my mum earlier. Looking around me, everyone seems to be having a great time, but I can't help that something, somewhere is wrong. Mal and Daisy seem relaxed as they sit side by side on the sofa. Outside, Heath and Max look deep in conversation; just their facial expressions alone have me curious as to the topic of their discussion, and Melissa. Well, she's just being Melissa. Sitting looking pretty while catching sneaky glances towards Heath when she thinks no one is looking. Honestly she couldn't possibly drool any more than she already is. I really hope that I don't look like that, when I'm checking Max out.

In such a short time, I'd like to think that I have become pretty close with Melissa and I'm really going to miss her when I have to go back home. Automatically my eyes lock onto Max as that thought passes through my mind. Yes, some things I am definitely going to miss. Thinking of home, I pull out my phone and send a quick message to Jen and George, when I notice another six missed calls from my mum. Jeez, is hurling abuse at me once already not enough for that woman? I swipe the screen and erase the missed calls. No way will I be calling her back anytime soon.

"More drama?" Melissa asks as she takes in my phone.

"No, nothing important anyway. I just wanted to

check in with Jen and George."

"I've been thinking." Now that doesn't sound too promising, I think to myself.

"What?" She asks when she sees my expression.

"I'm not sure in like the sound of that to be honest, Liss. It could be pretty dangerous."

"Very funny, bitch. I was just going to say, that I really hope I get to meet those two one day soon. Maybe when you and my brother make shit official and get married, hey?" She smiles. I almost choke on my drink at her words. No fucking way did those words just leave her lips.

"That's pretty optimistic Liss, even for you."

"Oh, believe me girly. If Max is going to marry someone, then rest assured that someone *will* most definitely be you."

"That definitely isn't going to happen. Who knows, it might be you and Heath that tie the knot. Now I'd happily invite them to see that." I watch as she splutters a little and her eyes pop open. "What? Surely it's not that bad?"

"That stupid, fucking bitch. What the hell is she doing here?" Before I have time to ask what, or who she means, Melissa is out of her seat and making her way out to the patio. My eyes automatically follow her and linger in that direction until they fall instantly on the hand that is placed on Max's arm. My eyes flitter from that hand and to Max, to try and sense some kind of reaction from him. He's stood quite causally and doesn't seem as pissed off as I would have expected him to look. I know that I have nothing to worry about, jeez everyone has told me as much, but I don't like seeing her touch Max at all. If I had my way then she would be out of his life forever and I know I'm being selfish, but the woman cannot be trusted.

It takes everything I have to stay seated at the table when all I want to do is head outside and make a stand. There is no way that I'm prepared to let her poison come between me and Max again. I have no idea why she would be turning up at Mal's house, anyway.

From where I sit, I watch closely as Melissa confronts her. Unfortunately I can't hear what she's saying, but to be honest, I'm not sure I want to. Whatever she has said must have hit a nerve, because she quickly turns on her heels and walks away. It's a shame she doesn't fall and cause herself and injury, the stupid fucking cow bag.

I feel Max's stare on me instantly, his eyes shining so bright that they burn into the depths of my soul. He looks at me with such a passion, that it hurts and his mouth curves into a delicious smile and I can't help but smile back at him. *My perfectly imperfect rogue, knocking me for six once again.*

The rest of the evening passes by without any further drama, thank god. Both Mal and Daisy seem to have enjoyed everyone's company immensely and they now sit out on the patio hand in hand looking happier than I have ever seen them.

"Hey." Melissa whispers as she sneaks up behind me, a little bit merry from the alcohol that she's consumed over the last few hours.

"Hey yourself." I whisper back to her. "Why are we whispering?"

"I have no idea. Me and Heath are gonna head off soon." A megawatt smile brightens her whole face at the mention of his name.

"Jeez, you've got it so bad. Go, go, get out of here then, you animal."

"Awesome. One last thing. Could you let Heath know

that I'll wait for him down the road, the last thing we want is Mr Moody catching us and ruining our fun."

"No way will Max overreact as much as you think he will. He's gonna be more pissed that you both kept it from him."

"Jess, I fucking love you. Really, really love you." Her hands grab my face as she kisses me on the lips. Slowly she pulls back to look at me, worry written all over her face. "I'm not ready for him to find out yet, okay? Please don't tell him and ruin this for me."

"Go on then, quickly before he comes over." I get that she's having the time of her life right now, but I don't like lies. If everyone was completely honest with each other, then people wouldn't get hurt as often as they do.

"You're amazing, Jess." I'm still laughing at her as she staggers to the door, while slurring her goodbyes to everyone, when I feel a strong, dominant presence behind me. I force myself to stay focused, but fucking hell it's hard.

Whenever he is near me I melt. His voice alone is hypnotic. His hand rests just over the curve of my backside as he leans in close to me.

"It makes me so fucking happy that you two get on so well."

"Yeah, she's a gem. I guess I've found my Jen away from home." I tilt my head slightly and look up to see him examining me with his eyes. His eyebrows hitch up a little, when he finally registers what I have just said. Without warning his head goes back on a laugh.

"Yeah, I can see it now. It's uncanny how familiar they are." His face turns softer as he bends his head down towards me. "Jess. It makes me happy to see *you* happy."

"What did Stella want, earlier?" The words fly out of my mouth before I have a chance to stop them. Me and my big fat gob, me and my big fat gob mixed with alcohol. *Way to go Jess.* Max's eyes darken and a frown creases his forehead very briefly and then a smile finds itself on his face again, as he looks at me.

"It was nothing important, angel."

"Oh." I reply, deeply disappointed with his answer. His tone sounded final and I decide not to press the issue any further. I just don't get why he won't tell me. I know that it's absolutely none of my business, but the other part of me is screaming to find out what that manipulating bitch is up to.

"Stella is definitely going to be an issue for me while I'm here you know?" There, I've said it a few times. Now it's up to him to decide how he plays this. I don't expect him to actually fire her, but I'd fucking love it if he did. My head is swiftly pulled up so that I am forced to look directly at him, his finger and thumb securely holding my chin in place so that I can't pull away.

"It wasn't important angel, okay? Stella isn't important. Shit, no one is important to me, not the way you are. Do you understand?"

Shitting hell. When he looks at me like that my head goes fuzzy and I lose all sense of everything completely, aside from the two of us in this little bubble.

"I said okay?" Max repeats his question while eagerly waiting for me to reply.

"Okay." Is all I manage to get out before his lips come crashing down against mine. Automatically the outside world separates itself from me and Max, as we search each other desperately, both of us wanting and needing more. His hand presses harder against the base of my spine, pulling me into him as close as he can get. My body is on fire once again, as I feel him harden against me. It takes every ounce of strength that I have to pull away as I remember our surroundings.

Fuck

I can't believe I have just allowed that to happen, at Mal's house of all places. As I slowly peel myself out of his arms a loud round of applause erupts around us.

"About bloody time too, I say." My eyes rest on Max, before I turn my head to the left to see both Mal and Daisy beaming at us with delight. Talk about embarrassing and I suddenly feel about twelve.

"Make sure you treat her properly Maxwell, otherwise it will be me that you'll be dealing with, you hear?"

"Maxwell?" I ask with a shy grin creeping across my face. Maybe I should call him Maxwell from now on. Judging from the discomfort written across his face I think I could have endless amounts of fun with it. Max's arms embrace me as I'm pulled in close. All I want right now is for the world to open up and swallow me whole, anything to stop my flustered face being watched by speculating eyes.

"Well I think it's lovely, dear and it's good that the two of you have made up. Just remember to let him know who's boss and you should be fine." Daisy's comment causes a laugh to break free, easing my embarrassment, a little.

"Oh, you can most definitely count on it." I smile as I take in the wonderful people around me and wonder just how long this feeling of euphoria will last.

"Are you ready to go?" I'm seated on the lounge chair discussing business with Mal, when Max interrupts me mid conversation.

"Go where?" I ask, slightly confused while his eyebrows shoot up as if to say, "*tell me you're not being serious?*"

"Come on. It's time for me to take you home." My hand is taken within his as I am pulled out of the chair and settled into his warm embrace. His manly smell that is so unique to him, is intoxicating. I don't truly think I will ever get my fill of him. I manage to say goodbye to Mal and Daisy just before Max begins ushering me down the driveway. He's bloody one dominating man, but I guess that's just Max and he is who he is, and in all honesty, I wouldn't change him for the world.

We walk in silence for a while, neither of us sober enough to drive. It's not an awkward silence, more of *a we're comfortable just stealing shy glances at each other* kind of silence, and it's nice. My hand is entwined within Max's and that contact alone has my skin breaking out in a heated glow.

"Where are we going?" I ask after sometime. Everywhere is still completely new to me, but at least Max is by my side leading the way.

"Always questions, angel." My heart flutters as his face shines brightly against the moonlight. He is absolute perfection. "Try and trust me just once?" His eyes plead for me to trust him and my heart smiles at that perfect, beautiful face of his. I'd love nothing more than to trust him fully, but he and I both know that I've been burnt too many times for that to happen.

After a few more minutes we stop at a path leading out to the ocean.

"Where are we?" I ask, me and my curious mind never stops.

"This is one of my favourite places. I usually come here when I need to think, or take a time out."

"So you spend a lot of time here, then?" His shoulders are set, his facial expression hard and serious. I remain silent as his mouth opens and closes a few times as if he wants to say something, but each time he decides against it.

"It's so beautiful here." I'm envious that Max gets to

experience this every day. I think if I were to live here permanently, there would be no way that I'd be able to get everything done that I needed to with all these gorgeous distractions.

"What happens next?"

"Hmm?" I'm barely listening as I imprint these breath taking images into my mind for an eternity.

"You and me angel. Where do we go from here? I can't and won't lose you again, no matter what. Fuck, I'm trying here Jess, but I told you I'm no fucking good at this shit."

My loveable rogue walks away from me with his hands running through his hair in frustration. I begin to walk towards him when he suddenly spins on his heels and turns back to me.

"Stay." It comes out more of a painful plea, than a question. Stay? What does he mean? I'm already at Melissa's and I'm happy there for now.

"I'm okay at Melissa's. Plus, she loves having another female around apparently. We've already been through how much your sister loves me." I laugh, a little bit tipsy from the alcohol that I've consumed. Max stalks forward towards me looking like a man on a mission. He gently places both hands on my face tenderly, before placing a chaste kiss on my lips and then onto my forehead.

"I mean... Fuck. Stay with me. Stay here permanently, goddamit."

"Max..." I begin but have no idea how I am going to end that sentence. What the hell does he expect me to say to that?

"I don't care what it takes, Jess. I need you. Fucking hell, even my home doesn't feel like home when you're not there. That's now much you affect me, how much you have changed me. I don't care how; all I know is that I need you with me."

Whoa. Where is all this coming from? As much as I would love to, I just can't give up my life back home for him at the click of his fingers, not matter how beautiful and imperfect he is.

"I can't just drop everything that I have ever known Max, not just like that."

"Why not?" His face remains impassive, while searching mine and his serious deep blue's burn right into me, pleading for me to give him the one answer that I can't.

"You're being deadly serious, aren't you?" Oh, fucking hell he is as well. I haven't got a clue where this is all coming from. He's going back and forth like a bloody yo-yo and I can't keep up with him.

"I've never been more serious about anything in my whole entire life, Jess. Fuck, I'll move back to London if that's what it takes."

"Don't be so stupid Max. There is no way that you're coming back to London, ever. Mal's finally settled here and I thought that's what you wanted."

"It was, it is. Shit, I just don't know any more, Jess. All I know is that I need to be with you, wherever you are. I just can't bear the thought of you walking out of my life, never to return again."

His hands are still cupping my face and I'm rendered speechless. For all of his beauty, he clearly has no fucking brains. I highly doubt he even knows what he's saying right now.

"You haven't known me long enough to drop everything Max. One day you will wake up and realise that it was the biggest mistake that you have ever made."

"No day with you could ever be a mistake, angel. Only the ones that I spend without you by my side."

Jess

I look over at the clock on my bedside table and see that it's just past midnight. No matter how hard I try, I just can't settle. The anxiety that has been eating away at me since the afternoon has me on edge and I have no idea why. Admitting defeat I slowly put my feet down on the floor and pull myself out of bed. Coffee. Coffee solves everything, so I make my way in that direction to the kitchen. Judging by the clothes that are scattered here and there, I think it's safe to say that Heath is currently occupying Melissa's bedroom. The kinky bitch.

As much as I wanted to stay with Max last night and as much as he pleaded for me to do so, I surprised myself by staying strong and just about resisted his charm. After his sudden declaration and proposition, all I wanted to do was clear my head and there would be no chance of that if I had taken him up on his very tempting offer. I also didn't want to jump back into *us* again with my eyes closed. Instead I quite proudly told him, "if you want this to work, we need baby steps. One day at a time and we'll see what happens." Needless to say, in true Max style, he didn't take it very well at all. It took half an hour of me pleading with him, to see my reasons behind it until he finally stopped spitting his dummy out.

If Max is going to be with me, then he needs to get used to hearing the word no. I know it's not going to be easy, but I guess nothing really is. The bloody stubborn man. In a way I've done nothing but punish myself really, because had I not have been so stubborn myself, I know that right now I would be either having hot wild sex, or deep in a slumber from said hot wild sex. As soon as I finish my coffee, I go back to my room and await the sleep that I need to overtake me.

There's no sign of Melissa as I finally come waltzing into the living area just after midday. There is also no living proof that Heath was here either. I'll give it to them both, they know how to clean up after themselves. Before I leave, one thing is for certain. If Melissa and Heath are as into each other as they make out, then she's going to have to tell Max. It's not fair for them to keep this from him. Maybe if they're upfront with him, he won't fly of the handle as much when they tell him. If Heath makes her happy, then I really don't see the problem. We're all adults here.

Men.

I don't think we will ever really understand them, but with that being said, do we really want to?

As soon as my coffee is freshly brewed I pull up at the island and pull out my phone hoping to see a message from Jen or George to relieve me from feeling so homesick. Swiping over the screen, all I see are my apps. No missed calls, no emails, Nothing. She's probably a little occupied with Luke, still I decide to send her an email. Maybe she can read it when she's not attached to his man piece.

Hey bitch,How are you? I'm missing you like crazy here and you can't even be bothered to call or send me a quick text. Paradise just kind of turned perfect. Me and Max are going to give it another go and see what happens. Baby steps, definitely baby steps this time.

He explained what happened with that psycho wench, yes I know, I know, I actually allowed him to talk. I'm still shocked at my kindness too.
How are things with Luke? You've been a bit quiet lately, so you're either constantly at it, or something has happened that you're keeping from me. I swear to god it better not be the latter because you know I will hunt you down.Well, call me when you can.
Love you xx

"I love how you look when you've just woken up, but it should be my bed where I first see you." My head snaps up at that voice instantly. The voice that can cause feelings within me that no other can.

"You shouldn't be here. We've been through this already and I thought that you had agreed." I point at him, yet secretly pleased that he has turned up out of the blue. I just pray that he doesn't decide to have a strop again. I don't think I can cope with two in twenty-four hours.

"If I remember correctly, I agreed to whatever made you happy and right now, I'd say your face looks pretty fucking happy."

"I'm happy..." I begin but I'm swiftly cut off as his mouth reaches mine, his stubble lightly grazing over my skin as he devours me whole and consumes me in every way. Mind, body and soul. He tastes of sun, coffee and Max which is a lethal combination and has me hungry for more, almost instantly. I pull back remembering my words from last night and I push half-heartedly against his chest, which in turn causes his hands to tighten within my hair a little bit harder.

"I've missed you, angel."

"You need to stop doing this." I whisper as soon as I pull myself fully out of his grasp. A frown forms across his face as he tries to figure out my meaning. "Trying to overrule everything I say."

"But angel, that's what I do. You say one thing and you know that I'm going to do the complete opposite. It's who I am."

Max

My eyes trail her every move as she steps around the kitchen. I'm not going anywhere without her no matter what she says, so I have made myself comfortable on the barstool. I can wait all day if I have too. She knows I'm not leaving until she is ready and she's taking her sweet arse time about it too. Who am I to complain with a view that fucking good? She really is something else and I fucking love the effect I have over her. Fuck, if only she knew what kind of effect she had over me. I have to push myself down to ease the fucking throb that she's caused by prancing around in shorter than short pants and her nipples fully erect through her skin tight vest top. I feel like I'm about to combust just from fucking looking at her. It's no good, I'm left with no choice but to try and re-arrange myself as she teasingly walks past me. Reaching out I grab hold of her waist and draw her in so that I can feel her perfect warm flesh against me.

"Don't even try to persuade me, Max." She laughs as I hold her tighter. I grab her hand and place it firmly on my crotch.

"You see how you fucking affect me, woman? You drive me fucking crazy and if I wanted to persuade you angel, you'd never have a chance to get away."

"Jeez. Leave the poor girl alone, Max. I'm all for a bit of PDA but I don't need bodily fluids all over my kitchen, guys." I instantly feel Jess try to pull away at Melissa's words, but I keep a firm hold on her.

"Calm down, Liss. Anyone would think you were a prude." The snort that comes from Jess at my words is so fucking cute. What the hell is this woman doing to me? I'm well and truly fucked?

"Okay, okay, let me go so I can get dressed. You happy now?" She asks as she turns to glare at me.

"Very." *More than you will ever know Miss Townsend*, I think to myself. "Be sure to pack your bikini." I shout after her.

"What's with the secrecy?"

"Hey?" I ask knowing full well what she means.

"Don't play dumb with me, Wild, where are you taking me?" Her perfect button nose wrinkles from the brightness of the sun and she looks so god damn good. I need to convince her and myself that this is what we need and we can do this, as long as we are in this together.

"Patience, angel. You'll soon see." I lean in and kiss her edible lips, lips that I could never tire of kissing and savouring. I can tell she's distressed, her posture is stiff and a scowl passes over her face. I've worked out that she hates the unknown, but with me that's something she's going to have to get used to and pretty fast. I don't do things by the book. Never have and never will. We walk for another fifteen minutes or so down the beach until we finally reach our destination. I cannot wait to see her face when she finds out what we'll be doing. You can't possibly come to the gold coast without experiencing this.

"Here we are, Miss." I say as we pull up to an information desk.

"I'm completely lost here Max. What's going on?"

"Have you ever been scuba diving, Jess?"

"Oh god no. Max I can't do this, please, please don't make me do this." She pleads. A look of pure terror on her face as a wicked one graces mine.

Jess

"I mean it Max. There is no bloody way I'm going in there." He thinks I'm joking, but this really isn't going to happen. Ever. I can't think of anything worse than swimming deep under water with only a tank to keep you breathing properly. I panic at the best of times, but this? "What if I forget to breathe? What if my tank doesn't work? Shit are you trying to kill me off?" He bursts out laughing at my panic and I can feel myself getting more and more worked up as time passes. "Angel, don't be silly. Do you really think I would let anything happen to you? I thought it would be romantic." He says as he gently runs his fingers through my hair, trying his best to calm me down.

Instantly my heart sinks as I realise he has put quite a lot of thought into this little adventure for us. Even calling it romantic is quite a big step for Max. Maybe I should at least try. "Would you mind if I snorkeled? I'll happily give that a go."

"You can do whatever you like. This trip is for both of us to try and relax and enjoy each other's company without any added pressure." He leans in as he runs his thumb along my jaw while looking directly into my eyes.

"Oh I like the sound of that, that sounds like fun. So what do we need to do now?"

"Well, you won't be needing any beginners training for snorkeling, so we can head straight to the yacht if you like, unless you want to do something else?" His face is so passive. What the hell, it's not like every day I get the choice to board a yacht. To be honest, I don't think I've even been on a boat since I was five and that was a family trip to Ireland. I can't keep the smile from my face as he leads the way.

"You look happy. I love it when you look happy."

"Yeah, I am. It must be all this vitamin d that I've soaked up into my body. That's about as exciting as this trip is." I'm rewarded with a swat to the arse for my cheek, before he takes my hand and leads the way.

As soon as we reach the yacht, I can't help but let out a massive "*WOW*." I've only ever seen a boat like this on MTV cribs. This stuff just doesn't exist in my normal day to day life.

"Jeez Max, it's a beast. Is everyone else on board already, or do we need to wait?"

"The only people that will be on this yacht, will be us two. No way will I be sharing you with anyone. Not today, not any day."

A shiver of excitement runs through my body at his words. I hope that I never, ever get my fill of this man. "I can't imagine what it must feel like to own a yacht. How do people possibly find the time to use it?"

"You want it angel, then it's yours. Anything that is mine is always yours to do as you please." My hands find themselves in his hair as I stand up on my tiptoes to thank him with a kiss. Oh how I want so much more, but for now a kiss will have to do.

It's surreal to know that Max has his very own yacht. What doesn't this man own? I guess I could say me, but I don't think that counts as a prized possession. The weather is perfect for our little trip. Nice and sunny with a subtle breeze and I'm glad I decided on cut off shorts and a vest top.

"Here you go." I look up to see Max standing over me with two pairs of snorkels in his hands. "I hope these are sufficient enough for you Miss Townsend?"

"Yes sir." I laugh and take in his body. He stands before me in just a pair of loose fitting swim shorts that fall just below the knees and expose his happy trail and that magical V shape that I struggle to resist so much.

"You ready to go in?" He asks, but I think I could sit here and admire his beauty all day and never get bored.

"What, now? I don't have any other clothes to change into."

"Did you not hear me call after you to pack a bikini?"

"Erm, no sorry." I was beaming with excitement to even contemplate anything else going on around me at his unexpected arrival this morning.

"Who said you need clothes to jump in, anyway? It's just you and me out here angel."

"Ha, nice try Mr. I'm not going further than my underwear or I'm staying here."

"Deal. But I can't promise that you'll come back out wearing anything." The wicked glint in his eyes gears me up for that challenge and before I can change my mind, I quickly get up and jump overboard. The water is bloody freezing and my skin feels like it's being attacked by a thousand needles as soon the impact hits my body. I feel something grab my hip and I scream out in a panic. Fuck what if it's a shark? Oh god, I'm going to die.

"It's me." The sound of Max's voice calms me a little but I'm still a little shaken.

"You little fucker. Don't ever do that again. I thought it was a shark about to eat me alive."

"You're the crazy loon who decided to fucking jump in without warning." He laughs. If we weren't in cold water and I didn't feel like I had to hold onto him, I'd wipe that cocky smirk off his bloody face, but I think he's fully aware that I need him right now. Before I know what's happening I'm being taken back to the yacht as I hold onto him as tight as I can. As soon as we reach our destination I'm pinned up against the ladders as Max takes full control over my body. It pointless fighting it, I've been holding back for too long and it's too exhausting so now, I finally allow my body to react and submit to his touch.

I've never been intimate with anyone in the ocean before, so this is definitely a first for me.

"I've missed feeling you against me, Jess. So fucking much." A soft moan escapes my lips as I feel him press against me just where I need him to be. I try to pull him in closer, but as soon as I do he pulls back and looks at me with a knowing smirk on his face.

"I'd love nothing more than to take you right here, right now, but I promised you a romantic snorkeling trip and I'd hate to break my promise to you." The bastard. He knows exactly what he's doing, working me up into a frenzy to then leave me hanging on.

"Max you can't do this to me. That's just cruel."

"Good things come to those who wait, angel." I wait for the punch line that doesn't come. Shit he's actually being serious. Well two can play that game, I think to myself as I reluctantly take the mask and snorkel from him. *Good things definitely do come to those who wait and Max wild is going to find he will be waiting for longer than he thought possible.* Who am I kidding, I'd be a fool to think that I could resist him.

I must admit that I actually enjoyed snorkeling with Max. He stayed by my side throughout it all, and even though he must have seen all of this in its beautiful glory a million times before, he took an interest and joined in my excitement every time I found something wonderful and new and I'll always be grateful to him for that.

"Are you hungry?" Max walks over to me in just a towel, as I stand drying myself off. Why does he have to look so goddamn hot all of the time? How is a girl supposed to think around here with such a beautiful distraction?

"A little bit. I'm sure I can wait until we arrive back though."

"Throw this on and follow me." His demand is plain and simple, followed by a look that dares me to argue with him. After the effort that he's put into all of this today, who am I to argue?

Now that he's mentioned food my stomach grumbles in agreement that it would like to be fed. I look at the garment that Max has just thrown to me and I'm surprised to see it's a basketball shirt. I'm thankful for the size as it's long enough to cover my secret parts and look like a dress. I leave my hair down, still slightly damp and follow Max out of the room.

As soon as I arrive back on the deck I see that a picnic has been placed before us. Max waits for me, now he has replaced his towel with some more shorts. He looks fresh from a cover shoot and I have to pinch myself that I'm actually here with him.

"Do you use this often?" I ask, signaling my surroundings. If I had a yacht, Jen would be inviting the whole of England to come and party on it weekly, if not every other night. She's going to freak when I fill her in on this little tidbit of information.

"Not as often as I used to, or as often as I would like. Why'd you ask?"

"I just wondered since you have clothes and toiletries on board."

"Everywhere I go Jess, I always have a spare toothbrush and a change of clothes." He says vaguely as he digs around in the basket for our feast.

"Oh." Is all I say and my mind whips back to when he pulled out a night bag from his car when he stayed over at mine. Obviously this must have been his little love boat and old habits die hard, I guess. I try not to let it bother me. I have no right to be bothered about anyone before me, as I didn't even know him back then, but it still niggles away at me.

"What's wrong Jess?" He must sense the change in my mood. I can't tell him that I'm suddenly overcome with jealousy at the thought of him with other women and that I'm pissed off that he would bring me to somewhere he uses for casual stuff. I try my best to smile at him but he sees straight through it.

"Nothing, I'm fine."

"Jess, one thing that's gonna piss me off real quick, is if you start lying to me. If you want to say something, then say it. I can't fucking read your mind."

"Did you used to bring other women here?"

"What? Where's that suddenly come from?"

"I don't know." I whisper suddenly feeling like a scolded child. "I just thought I would ask. I'm curious I guess."

"I would never bring you to a place that I have shared with another woman, Jess. You mean far too much to me to do that to you."

"What about the clothes? The toiletries."

"I told you. I always carry spares." He looks at me as if I have suddenly grown two heads, completely unaware of what I am getting at.

"But why? Why would you carry 'spares' all the time? Do you just go out and if it happens it happens?"

I can't help myself now. My backs up and there's no bringing it back down until I get an answer, no matter what it may be.

"You think I carry spares in case I get off with someone? Shit Jess, no. That's not what it is at all. I've always carried spare clothes on me since me and Liss were young. We never knew where we would end up from one day to the next. We moved around... A lot.

Sometimes we had nowhere to go and that's when the supplies came in handy. I've never took a single day for granted since and I guess it's my comforter to know that I have it. If ever I should need it again, then I have the essentials to get me through."

Wow. Well now I feel like a complete heartless bitch that jumps to conclusions that couldn't be any further from the truth. I knew something must have happened to him when he was younger, I just didn't know that it was bad enough to leave such deep scars.

"Max I'm sorry I shouldn't have pried into your personal business..."

"Don't apologise for something you don't know about, Jess. I'm good, it's just habit that's all and like they say, old habbits die hard. Now if you've finished with your questions for at least half an hour, maybe we could eat?"

"Perfect, sounds like a plan to me." I crawl over to him to prevent any void from taking place after that little discussion. Today has been perfect so far, and I'd hate to cause any issues that don't need to be there.

The sun is still out and it's a nice temperature with a subtle breeze, where I lie sunbathing. All that swimming has completely worn me out. As soon as Max begins to rub oil into my shoulder, I feel that relaxed that I could quite easily take a nap. Max slowly and gently kneads the muscles in my back and then slowly brings them around down the side of my breast in delicate circular motions. Almost instantly I can feel a dull ache begin to build up in my core. Unable to take the pressure, I push back against the palm of his other hand that is busy kneading my arse and try and ease the ache. I roll over onto my back so Max gets better access to my front and where I really need him to be.

"If you stayed, we could spend most days like this

together. Just you and me, secluded where no one else could interrupt us."

"I like the sound of that." I'm unable to concentrate as Max expertly explores beneath my bikini bottoms, teasing and rubbing me in a perfect rhythm. My hips begin to move as he picks up the pace and just as I can feel my release getting closer and closer, his warm mouth closes around me as he strokes me on the inside and teases me with his mouth and tongue on the outside. My legs stiffen around him as I feel the assault of ecstasy take over my body and I begin to pant his name while gripping tightly onto his hair. Shitting hell this man is utterly perfect in every possible way.

When he finally comes back up and looks at me, he slowly leans down against me and I curl into him, holding onto him as tight as I can and silently thank him for such a perfect day.

Jess

We arrive back at Melissa's shortly after six and I'm still beaming from the perfect day that I've had with Max. I've seen the softer side to him previously, but today was like nothing that I'd ever experienced before. He's so tentative and caring and nothing was ever too much for him.

"Oh and the love birds finally return. Did you have fun?" Melissa chimes to life as soon as we walk through the door.

"It was perfect." A massive grin spreads across my face as Max gives my hand a little squeeze.

"Well it's alright for some, I suppose. I've been bored shitless."

"Really? I somehow find that hard to believe, you've always got something stuffed up your sleeve." I wonder if Heath has been hanging around while the coast has been clear. Just as I'm about to plonk my arse on the barstool my phone chimes to life in my bag. As soon as I see the caller I.D, panic begins to swirl within my chest. I answer it instantly and hold my hand up to Liss and Max to quieten down a minute.

"Hi Tim. How are you?" I try to listen to his panic stricken voice on the other end of the line but he's talking way to fast and I can't understand him. "Okay, calm down. Start right from the beginning and slowly, so that I can try to understand you."

"Where to start Jess, where to fucking start. Everything's gone tits up. I wanted to call you sooner, really I did but what with Mal's ill health, I didn't want to cause any more drama, but enough is enough. I can't take it anymore."

"What's happened? What do you mean everything's gone tits up?"

"Stanton's. Something has happened to one of the backup files for one of the major clients. I haven't got a fucking clue how it fix it. The phones are ringing off the hook as all the designs are lost too. Someone from that business is threatening to go to the press for breach of data protection."

"How?" I am hearing everything that he's saying, but none of it is making any sense whatsoever.

"Someone, somewhere has removed the file and it has all of their sensitive information on it. I don't know how, but it's managed to get back to some of them and now the shit has well and truly hit the fucking fan. Oh Jess we're screwed. What the fuck am I supposed to do?"

"Fuck. Right let me see what I can try and find out, and I'll come back to you ASAP okay?"

"Thanks. I'm so sorry to drop this on you."

"Don't worry about it; I'll speak to you soon. Try not to panic, we'll sort it if we can." I say to him, when all I'm really doing is panicking on the inside. Why can nothing ever go right, just once?

Shit, shit, shit. How the hell has this happened? Mal's going to hit the roof. He can't find out the extent of this, otherwise he'll definitely end up back in hospital.

"Jess what's going on? You've gone white." I look at Melissa but I can't seem to get the words out. Instead I just stand in front of Liss and Max waiting for a resolution to pop out of thin air, but I know that I'll be waiting for a bloody long time without anyone's help.

"Jess, what did he say?"

"It's... It's Stanton's. They're in deep shit."

I relay the information Tim has passed onto me to Max and wish I hadn't. He looks furious, deadly even. Melissa looks like she understands, but I actually don't think she does to be honest.

"What am I going to do?"

"Mal mustn't find out. From any of us, am I clear?" Both me and Melissa nod in sync to Max's demand. "You won't be doing anything, *we* - me and you together will sort this okay? Don't get yourself worked up over it. There's not much we can do right now anyway, not until we have more information on it."

"Are you kidding me? I need to go back and sort this mess that they've suddenly found themselves in. How on earth have they managed to lose this super sensitive file?"

"Trust me Jess, that's the first thing that I'll be finding out. Believe me."

"Maybe it could have been hacked?" Melissa chimes in and she actually has a valid point. Max is quick to shoot it down though.

"It's a possibility, but a very slim one. Me and Mal have been using the same security for years and it's the most secure that there is."

I really don't like the sound of this, one bit. We bloody leave the office for a few weeks and all hell breaks loose. I try to call Amelia to see what has been happening since I have been gone, but it just goes to voicemail. Why is no one answering there phones when I bloody need them to the most?

"Hey Tim, it's Jess." I say as he answers on the first ring.

"That was quick, can it be fixed? Please god tell me it can be fixed."

"I really wish I could Tim. I've got Max in on it from this end. I need you to think back and tell me everyone who has access to the main drives. I'm going to need dates and times so we can see if there has been any dodgy activity on any of the accounts."

"Sure. I should be able to get that for you. What else do you need me to do?"

"Book me a flight out, one back to Heathrow tomorrow. I don't care what time, we just need to get this mess sorted, ASAP."

"Okay, will do. I'll email you the flight confirmations as soon as I have them."

"Brilliant. One last thing before I go, could you get Amelia to call me. All I keep getting is her voicemail and I need to speak to her urgently."

"That might be a bit tricky seeing as though she has been off sick since Mal flew out." Honestly could this mess get any worse?

"Okay well if you speak to her before I do, get her to call me please. Okay, thanks. Bye Tim."

I put the phone down to be greeted with two sets of eyes burning holes into me.

"What?" I say suddenly, conscious I have something unsightly on my face.

"You are not going back home Jess. This isn't your mess to fix."

"Of course it is. I work there and I have built most of these clients up on my own, Max. I'm leaving tomorrow and that's final."

"Over my fucking dead body. If I have to keep you here I will do. You've got work to do here."

"Excuse me?" I can't believe he has just thrown that line on me. "Yes I may work here for *now* Max, but Stanton's is my career and where my priorities are. I will not sit back and watch all of Mal's hard work crumble and collapse around him. I thought you would have felt the same."

"Okay guys, maybe we should calm down a little. All of this shouting isn't going to solve the situation, is it?" As much as I hate to admit it, Melissa has a point. I stare at Max head on, adamant in my plans.

"I will leave tomorrow and I don't want to hear another word about it."

Max

I stand and watch the lights flicker before me. I love it when the house is all lit up ready for Christmas. I hear his voice first and instantly feel bile begin to rise in my throat. What is *he* doing here? He shouldn't be here anymore, not after what *he* did. My first thought goes straight to Melissa. Shit, I hope she's not here. Please let her be anywhere but here. That's when my blood suddenly runs colds and turns to ice. Jess' laugh sounds out in the distance. Please no, not Jess. Don't let him near my Jess. I try to run towards the sound of her voice but my legs won't move fast enough. With each step that I take, her voice seems to get farther and farther away.

"Jess, Jess where are you?" I cry out, desperate for her to reply. She doesn't answer me. Why isn't she answering me? All I can hear is her laugh but she doesn't say anything.

I round the hallway and stop in the living room, and that's when I see him. He stands, just like he always used to, still wearing the same battered tartan shirt and smelling of sweat and alcohol.

"Jess." I call out again but she doesn't turn. Instead all I see is him as he turns slowly to face me.

"So good to see you again Max. My, my how you have grown." His greasy hair is combed back and his grin causes chills of dread to shiver down my spine. This can't be happening. How the hell has he got here?

"What are you doing here? You know you shouldn't have come back, not after last time." Anger fills up inside me and the memories suddenly resurface from the very last time that I saw him. I swear if he touches a single hair on her head, I'll make sure I do what I should have fucking done years ago without a moments fucking hesitation. This time he won't walk away without paying for his actions.

"That's no way to greet your old man now, is it *son*?"

"I'm not your son. Don't you ever call me your son, you murdering bastard." His right arm swiftly curves around Jess' neck and I hear a click. A whimper escapes her lips as she suddenly realises what's about to happen, my eyes zoning in on the gun that's been placed at her temple.

"You're just like her you know. Right down to your fucking arrogance and stubbornness. Only she knew when to fucking keep quiet." He looks at Jess and reaches out to touch her hair. "She's a bit too pretty for you, isn't she Max? It's a shame it's all going to go to waste." I hear another click and scream out as the gunshot sounds around the room, penetrating my mind to remind me what happens when I become weak.

"Nooooooo.... Jess!" I try to scream but the words freeze on my lips.

My eyes shoot open and all I can see is darkness around me. I'm covered in sweat and the sheets cling to my cold damp body. I try to regulate my breathing but all I can see in my mind is Jess on the floor in a heap, while the life is drained completely from her body.

"*It's just a dream, just a fucked up, fucking dream.*" I repeat over and over but it felt so fucking real and every thing was laid out just like last time, only now he had Jess as his victim. Leaning out to grab my phone, I see that it's just gone 3am. I don't think twice about the time, I just need to hear her voice and to make sure that she's okay. The call goes straight to voicemail. *What are you doing Max? She'll be asleep.* Knowing full well that sleep is not going to happen for me, I lower my feet to the floor and try to compose myself.

"I can get there for ten. Yeah that's fine, I'll see you then." I still can't shift the image of Jess lying before me out of my mind. I need to get these nightmares under control. I've been for a surf and ran a couple of miles on the treadmill and nothing is easing up the fear that is niggling away at me. The fear of losing another person that I care about at the hands of that evil bastard. I have no idea why he is suddenly penetrating my dreams after all this time, but I don't fucking like it. I try Jess again, the sudden need to speak to her driving me insane. It still goes to fucking voicemail so I call Melissa instead.

"Hey Max. What's up?"

"I'm trying to get hold of Jess but it keeps going to voicemail. Is she around?"

"Erm..." She says after a pause.

"Where is she Liss?" I demand, trying to hold back from lashing out at her, from my frustration.

"She's on her way back home. She told you yesterday."

"What the fuck? I told her that she wasn't to leave until we had this shit under wraps. Fuck, when did she leave? What the fuck were you thinking letting her go?"

"I've no idea. I woke up to her note this morning. She said she'll call when she lands. What's up your arse anyway? I can't keep her here against her will, Max."

"If she calls you when she lands make sure you tell her to call me, you understand?"

"I don't know what's happened, but learn to fucking talk to me properly Max."

"Hey Liss, I'm sorry. Do me a favour, hey? Stay safe."

"Umm. Okay. You're weirding me out, but can do." I slam the phone down in frustration. Why the fuck can't people just listen to me? Life would be so much fucking easier all around for everyone involved.

Jess

I still can't get hold of Amelia. I don't know what she's playing at, but I'll make bloody sure I do when I land. She told me she could handle the workload, but as soon as I leave she's off sick. What's that about? I knew she'd been having problems but still. I'll hold my hands up and apologise for being a bitch if she's genuinely ill, but to me something sounds off and I'll make it my mission to find out what if I have to once I have dealt with this other drama.

I can't believe Tim has been left to deal with most of this on his own either. I dread to think how far this could have gone if he hadn't have called. The aim of the game is to have this little situation resolved before Mal finds out or worse, before his pride and joy falls down the shitter.

This flight is going to be the longest one of my life. In the mad rush, I didn't think about what I would need, so as soon as Tim called and told me that there was a flight due to leave in a few hours I didn't hesitate and left for the airport. I did remember to leave a note for Liss, but I know Max is going to hit the roof. I guess I'll just have to deal with that crazy whirlwind when the time comes. All that I can do now is dig out my headphones and watch whatever they decide to show throughout the journey.

Max

"Mr wild. Please come this way." I look up to the tall leggy blonde before me. In the past she would have been right up my street, but not anymore. Sure she's pretty but she seems to lack the kind of class that surrounds Jess. She's completely ruined me for anyone else. I walk into the office and feel the same apprehension that I felt the last time, but now things are getting completely out of hand.

"Max." Don nods at me as I take a seat on the sofa before him. "Glad to have you back. Will you be staying this time?" My head falls into my hands as I realise how out of control my life has become in the past few weeks. I never asked for any of this shit.

"I need help Don. It fucking kills me to admit it, but I do. I can't go on like this anymore. Whatever it is you need to do, just do it. I need to be fixed."

Unfolding his legs, he leans forward to examine me closely. A look of uncertainty mixed with disbelief, I'm not too sure passes over his face and then it's gone just as fast as it came. "

"Are you ready to tell me what's eating at you?"

"The nightmares have retuned. I can't sleep with the intensity of them. It's getting to a point where it's affecting my day to day life."

"What kind of nightmares? Are we taking flashbacks?" He asks, his attention firmly on me.

"Flashbacks would be more liveable. It's like I'm reliving all the bad moments again and again, only know it's mixed up with the present." Fucking hell. What good is this doing me? Sat here pouring my heart and soul out to look like a fucking pussy once again.

"You said last time that this started again after you travelled back to England? Do you think something there could have been a trigger for you?"

"No. Maybe, oh I don't know. Living in England was always my safe place Don. You know this already." I watch him as he riffles through my file, looking for something, but what I'm not so sure.

"Ah yes' here it is. How is Melissa these days?"

"She's fine. Why?"

"Do the nightmares have a pattern? After specific events or when you spend time with a specific person?"

"How the hell am I supposed to remember that? All I know is that they're getting more and more frequent with each day that passes. Now it's getting to the fucking point where *he's* penetrating my dreams, threatening to take away my only true piece of happiness."

"Is that what you're worried about, Max? This one piece happiness, did she come into your life before these feelings started to return?"

"Does it matter?" My heads fucked. I don't really see how Jess being in my life could make such an impact. "Can you fix me or what?"

"I can give you something to help you sleep, but these issues that you're facing Max, I can't help you unless you are prepared to face them head on." For Jess, I'll do whatever it fucking takes to keep her safe from my past and also that vile bastard who ruined it all for us.

"You can count on it Don. I'll be out of town for a few weeks, but I'll schedule another meeting once I'm back."

I leave Don's office not sure I have resolved anything. Maybe once I get some of these pills in me and have a decent night's sleep, I'll feel better.

"Max, hey. I didn't think you'd be back after your dramatic exit last time." Sasha smiles at me as I walk past reception.

"Hey yeah. I guess that wasn't my best move, hey?"

"You didn't call. I've missed you Max, it's been too long." Her eyes light up expectantly, waiting for my response. Now really isn't the time to be getting into this. Jess has gone back home against my wishes, Mal's business is on the line and I need to get to the bottom of my issues. I know I'm a heartless bastard, that's old news, but I need to do this. I don't have the time nor the patience to be stood here right now.

"Sash listen. I've got some major shit taking off right now, hence why I'm here and I can't stop and chat. I'll catch up with you next time I'm here, but I wouldn't read anything into it if I were you. I'm not into all that casual shit anymore." Her jaw opens in shock but nothing comes out and I take that as my cue to leave.

"Max where are you?" Liss' tone sounds panicked on the other end of the line. "I've been trying to call you for the past hour."

"Have you heard from Jess? Is she okay?"

"Max, she's still in the air. Mal's been calling here asking for her and I've had to tell him she's headed home because of a family issue so we need to get our stories straight, so he doesn't start jumping to conclusions."

"Okay, shoot. What did you tell him? I'm on my way to his now, so be as quick as you can."

"Well, when we went to Mal's party last week her mum called and she was pretty shitty to her in a way that no mother should speak to their child. She was pretty upset, but she tried to hide it. Don't ever tell her I told you this okay? I told Mal that she needed to rush back to her mum but didn't say why and now I'm worried I've done the wrong thing Max."

"Don't worry about it. Just so I'm clear. Jess' mum called on Friday and she was upset and she's had to rush back for some reason?" Shit what issues has she been having with her mum. I had no idea and she didn't even tell me.

"You got it. But Max, promise me you won't tell her I told you that? I don't think she'd be too happy with everyone knowing."

"I promise. Remember if you hear from her, call me ASAP. I'll come to yours once I've been to Mal's." I click the call off and put my foot down and take off to Mal's. I need to find a way to go after Jess without raising any suspicions.

As I pull up outside the house, I have to go over again in my head what I'm going to say. I hope Daisy's not around; I never could get away with lying to her. As I walk through to the living room, Mal's positioned in his favourite chair looking better than ever, watching the television.

"Max my boy. It's good to see you. I guess you've heard about Jess then?"

"Yeah. Liss said she had to leave last night without a moment's notice."

"I hope everything's okay. Jess and her mum have never really seen eye to eye from what I can remember, but it must be bad if she's rushed off. Anyway while your here I may as well run it past you too."

Settling down on the sofa I look at him to continue, unsure of where this is leading. "Go on..."

"I've been doing a lot of thinking while I've been sat here this past week. What with my ill health, it's highly unlikely that I'll be able to fly for a while and I was hoping to talk to Jess about Stanton's."

"What about it?" There is no way he could know about the security breach, no fucking way.

""I always planned to hand the business over to her when I fully retired, but now my time has been pushed forward. What do you think of me making her a permanent CEO for Stanton's? She'd have to work here for 6 months of the year and then 6 months in the U.K."

"I think she'd bloody love it. She loves Stanton's, you know that."

"Yeah I do. It would have been nice to propose it to her face to face, though." Mal is an absolute fucking genius and he doesn't even know it.

"You still can. Why don't you ask her when she comes back? I was thinking while she's over there I could join her and check in on Stanton's. Everything's good with the development on this side. Thanks to Jess we're way ahead of schedule."

"You know Max, that sounds like a great idea. I'd appreciate you checking in and make sure you keep an on that special girl of mine." I smile knowingly at Mal. It seems he's always had a bit of a soft spot for Jess. Shit who doesn't?

"You betcha."

"It's good to see you happy, son. It's about bloody time too if you ask me." The pride on his face makes me feel like a little boy again, always receiving his praise no matter what I did.

"Thanks Mal. She's something else entirely." I laugh.

"Max dear, would you like something to eat?" Daisy asks as she pops her head around the door, her smile visible ear to ear.

"I'm good, but thanks anyway. I best get going if I want to catch a flight out today. Is there anything specific that you want me to keep an eye on while I'm there?"

"Just make sure the guys are working as well as they normally do and that all the accounts are up to date."

"Sure thing boss." I nod as I get up to leave. "I'll call you when I'm there."

The first thing I do as soon as I leave the house is call the airport to see what available flights they have going out to Heathrow. I must have done something fucking right as they have a seat available for first thing tomorrow morning. It's not soon enough, but shit, it will do.

"Liss, you here?" I shout out to the silent house before me. "Hello." I shout again.Still I get no answer. It's not like Liss to go out and leave her door unlocked. Maybe she's in the shower or some shit, so I'll sit here and wait until she shows up. After about ten minutes or so I hear Liss' high pitched laughter coming from the hallway. I go to shout her again to let her know that I'm here when she comes barreling into the kitchen in nothing but a towel with fucking Heath hot on her heels. Their faces drop as soon as they see me sitting here.

"Fuck, fuck fuck." Melissa hisses. "Max what are you doing here? Do you not know how to call or maybe knock before you come in?" She snarls.

Now there's a guilty fucking conscience if ever I saw one.

"What the fucks this?" I ask, signaling the two of them in nothing but towels. I eye Heath instantly. "You wanna tell me what's going on here, mate?"

"We went for a surf earlier and we've just got back. Thought I'd get changed, you know?" The casual tone in his voice has me riled up in no time.

"You expect me to believe that bullshit? Do you think I haven't noticed how you two have been acting around each other lately? Fucking hell Heath, I thought the two of you would finally grow some balls and admit what's been going on. I guess not, hey?"

"You're not angry?" Melissa asks as she looks at me in disbelief.

"Nah, I'm not angry. I'm pissed you didn't tell me, but I get it. Fuck her around Heath and then you'll see angry." I warn.

Anyone dating my sister is going to piss me off, but if it's someone I know and trust I can't really interfere. She's an adult and I guess she has to learn from her own mistakes. But if he so much as hurts a hair on her head, mate or not, I'll fucking kill him.

"Um, well this is all starting to feel a little awkward so I'm gonna go and stick some clothes on. I'll be back in five. Oh and Max..."

"Yeah?" I ask as she turns to face me.

"I love you."

"Quit with the soppy shit, I've got plans to make and I need both of you on this okay?"

Jess

I finally land on home turf after what feels like an eternity. All I want is my own bed and that's exactly what I'll be doing as soon as I leave this airport. Heathrow is bursting at the seams as usual and it smells like home. I didn't bring any luggage so at least I don't need to faff about waiting for anything. As soon as I'm past customs I call for a taxi to pick me up. I would have called Jen or George but it's six in the morning and I can't be bothered running through the drama straight away. When they chew my ears off later, I need to have some strength in me.

Everything looks just the same when I walk through the door. It even smells the same and a feeling of happiness swims through my body. I don't think twice as I step into my bedroom and dive into my ready and waiting bed. It's been a long thirty hours and as soon as my head hits the fluffy pillows I feel myself drifting instantly as I allow the darkness to consume me.

My eyes are heavy and sore as I try to open them. I don't know how long I have slept for, but it doesn't feel long enough. It takes me a few seconds to figure out where I am. As my eyes slowly adjust to the room around me, I realise that I'm home. I stretch out in my own bed and it feels bloody good. Well it does until I remember why I've come home. Ugh I don't know where I'm going to start. Do I tackle Amelia first or should I at least call Tim to let him know that I'm back and we can create some kind of plan.

I drag myself out of bed and my muscles ache so bad. I don't think I'm built for this jet lag shit and to make it worse I don't have Max to hold my hand this time. Oh fuck. At the thought of Max, I feel a pang of regret at just ditching him without a moment's notice and not saying goodbye. He's going to flip his shit. Well it's not like I have to face him for a while and it's highly unlikely that he'd fly halfway across the world to give me a stern telling off anyway.

As the hot water sprays down on me, I try to devise a plan but I'm coming up blank. I'm praying we can just get one of the I.T guys to retrieve the file and have done with it, but something tells me it's much bigger than this. Surely it couldn't have been an inside job. How else would the client have found out if they hadn't been given a tip off? As harsh as it sounds, I don't even think we have anyone with those kind of brains at Stanton's. If we did, then they've done a bloody good job of hiding it.

"Hey Tim, its Jess. How's things?"

"Oh Jess, what are we going to do? The client is making some pretty hefty demands and I don't have a fucking clue what to do about it."

"Well I'm back now. How about you come over to mine and we can try and figure something out. Who knows maybe there could be a trail of some sort to lead us to the culprit?"

"Wait, you think someone has done this deliberately?" I don't know why he sounds so shocked.

"Tim we live in a very competitive workplace darling, and sometimes competitors will take you by the balls no matter what the consequences."

"At times you scare me with that mind of yours, Jess. I'll be over within the hour."

As I wait for Tim to arrive, I spend my time going through the mail that has collated on my door mat. When I got in this morning I didn't even notice it, but now there's easily thirty or so letters to get through. No doubt most of them will be junk, but I've got to get through them eventually.

Well that's half an hour that I'll never get back. All my mail consisted of bills for Josh and takeaway menus and not forgetting the latest deals down at gala bingo over the next month. Maybe I should save that for George when I see him. He'd bloody love that. I can't wait to meet up with those two; I just need to get this situation under control first of all before I can enjoy some downtime with my besties.

When Tim turns up, I actually fall in love with him all over again. As he walks through the door my eyes dart to the Starbucks bag in his hand.

"I take it you haven't had a chance to grab something to eat and I know you don't function without coffee."

"Tim, remind me why we're not married." I laugh as I remember how bare my cupboards are.

"Oh Jessica love, if only you had the right toolkit." I lean in for a hug, suddenly realising how much I have missed him.

"I'm sorry you've had to deal with all this shit on your own Tim. I wish you would have called me sooner you know."

"You know me Jess. If there's one thing I hate, it's admitting defeat. Especially when it's something major that I have been entrusted to look after." He passes me my cappuccino along with a ham salad and my stomach grumbles, letting me know that it is in desperate need of some fuel.

"You know that no one, least of all Mal is going to

blame you for this? Whatever it is, we'll get to the bottom of it so I wouldn't worry too much. As long as we stick both of our heads in right, we'll get to the bottom of it. Mal doesn't know about any of this, by the way."

We eat in silence for a while, or at least Tim allows me to eat before he fills me in on what's been happening since I've been away.

"So, she's just been turning up as and when she pleases?" I say in disbelief. It's completely out of character for Amelia to hang her career on the line like this.

"Not to begin with. Some day's she'd be fine and others she would be an emotional wreck. I heard her arguing on the phone a few times to her boyfriend or whatever she wants to call him. To tell you the truth, if someone makes you cry like that, no way should they have the title of boyfriend attached to them. He sounds like a complete head fuck."

"Yeah, I think she was having a few problems with some guy before I left. The poor girl. I told her if she ever needed to talk to come and find me. So where is she now?"

"Who knows? You never know if she's going to make it in or not. Sometimes she comes in and then goes back home without a moment's notice. I can't cope with it anymore Jess, but I don't have the power to start any kind of disciplinary meetings and she knows she has me by the balls, or at least until Mal finds out anyway."

"Try and get hold of her for me. I think it's high time we had a little catch up. I just want to get to the bottom of why she's being so out of character."

Stanton's is dead. The whole vibe that I used to get a buzz off every day has vanished.

"Jeez Tim, it feels like it's sucking your energy from

your body. How the hell has it gotten this far? When was the last time the cleaners came out?"

"The last I heard, they turned up and Amelia sent them away because she had to head off in a hurry." Fucking hell. Old magazines are scattered around reception and it feels cold and dark.

"You, go stick that kettle on and fetch some bin bags and we'll make a start on trying to get this place back to normal." I try to call Amelia but yet again I have no luck. The longer this goes on the more pissed off I'm becoming.

As soon as I get into the swing of things, I feel my mood improving somewhat.

"Have meetings been taking place here in this state?" I ask as the thought suddenly dawns on me.

"I've tried to make sure that all meetings have been offsite until I could arrange someone to come in and sort it out."

"Well it's done now, at least." I'm still baffled how an office can get so disorganised in such a short space of time. "I think we need to buckle down and decide who actually wants to work for Mal and keep his baby soaring."

"I agree." Tim says as he plonks his arse down on a reception chair. "I meant to ask, but I thought I'd give you some headspace for a while."

"Ask away..." I say, fully aware of what's going to pop out of his mouth.

"How was Oz? Why were there no snaps on facebook?"

"Because my dear friend, I was too busy working to be talking selfies. But in all honestly, it's amazing. It's completely out of this world. I mean who do you know that wakes up to a beautiful beach every morning?"

"Alright bitch, you don't need to rub it in that much. What's happening with tall dark and handsome?"

"Who Max? It's hard to tell right now. We're both still kind of figuring out where we want this to go. Well at least we were until I came back home without telling him."

"I bet he's one pissed off puppy. How many times has he been on the blower?" Tim's comments remind me that I actually haven't heard from him at all since I left. He must be really pissed at me to not even call. Normally if I've made him angry my phone is blowing up with calls and texts.

"I've not heard from him. I don't know if that's a good thing or not. Well I've got this to keep me occupied for now."

"The least you could do is drop him a quick message to let him know that you got here safe." Good point, maybe I should.

I pick up my phone and type out a quick message to him. Hopefully Liss puts in a good word for me.

"Have you been onto the I.T guys?" I ask Tim, quite anxious to get the ball rolling. Josh would have been the perfect guy for the job, but no matter how much I want to get this resolved, there's no way I'm going to be asking him for help.

"I logged it last night as an urgent case, so hopefully they'll be in touch with an update soon.

"Let's hope so. What's happening with the accounts? I think I'll tackle those next." I'm fully centered in my to do mode and can't seem to stop. When I get hold of the person responsible for this, and yes I'm adamant there is someone behind this, god fucking help them.

"Right well, if you need me I'll be in the office." I leave Tim by reception and set of in the direction of my office. Thankfully this seems to be in one piece. It could do with a quick dust, but I guess that can be done later. I fire up the computer and bring up the programs that I need. Shit, should I even be using this if it's been hacked?

"Tim." I call out. He's at my door in seconds. "How many accounts has this happened to? Maybe I shouldn't go into the server in case something else gets taken?"

"As far as I'm aware, it's just one of the major ones and nothing else seems to have been affected."

"Do you think I should open it or wait 'til I.T. get back to us?"

"I'd definitely play it safe and wait until I.T. come back to us. If we have been hacked we could potentially be opening ourselves up to all sorts of shit."

I make a few calls to see if I can chase anything up, but everything seems to be going in slow motion. How hard can it be for bloody professionals to get to the bottom of such a critical incident? Deciding that nothing else can be done today, I head out to grab a much needed coffee and I'm overjoyed when I hear the voice of one of my faves.

"Princess." George comes barreling towards me as I walk through the door at Joes. I'm picked up off my feet within seconds and whirled around so fast that I feel dizzy. "Why didn't you tell me you were home? When did you get back?"

"I've missed you too." I say as I wait for him to lower me back to the ground. "Early this morning. I haven't has a chance to tell anyone yet. Let's just say the shit has well and truly hit the fan."

"Am I gonna have to work these muscles on some bell end from Australia?"

"No, not that kind of drama. Purely work stuff."

"Well I'm about to take a break so I'll bring your usual over, go get yourself a seat."

I look around and see that my favourite seat is available, tucked away in a little alcove next to the windows. I used to love dropping in here just to watch the world pass by.

"Here you go princess." I take my cappuccino from him as he pushes a chocolate chip brownie my way too. "What's a bit of gossip without chocolate?"
I laugh at my best friend. No matter what the situation he's always there to help me, plus with the mention of gossip it's hard to keep him away.

"It's good to be back, but I'm bloody shattered."

"How come you're not still living the life of Riley? I didn't expect you to be back for quite a while, to be honest."

"You know me George, I can't go for long without good old drama creeping up and biting me on the arse sooner or later." I wait for a smart arse comment, but nothing leaves his mouth. Instead he nods his head as if to say *"go on..."*

"I received a call from Tim the other day and he was in a right state and I couldn't work out why he was calling at first. When he finally calmed down he told me that Stanton's had landed deep in the shit. One of the major client's files has gone missing from the server along with all its super sensitive information on it. I haven't got a clue what I'm going to do about it and to make it worse, the client has somehow found out and are now threatening to out Mal and Stanton's."

"Shit. What took Tim so long to call you?"

"Oh I don't know. Maybe he thought he had everything under control or something. He's petrified of Mal finding out, that's why I ended up coming back as soon as I could."

"You know he's going to find out sooner or later, princess." He states.

"I know. I'm just praying for a miracle before that happens." As if I don't already know that I'm fighting a losing battle. Jeez George is supposed to be on my side.

"So come on then. Don't keep me waiting in suspense."

"Hmm." I ask completely oblivious to what he's asking me. My minds all over the place and I can't stop my mind from wandering off and over thinking things.

"The mystery woman, you know the *who is she* scenario. I'm guessing it wasn't his wife after all. I bloody hope it wasn't because I would have expected this conversation to have happened much sooner than now."

"Oh, you mean Stella?" Her name leaves a horrible taste in my mouth. I hate the thought of that vindictive bitch being around Max while I'm gone, patiently waiting to try and sink her claws into him once again.

"Judging by that face, I'd say you're a huge fan?"

"Seriously George, she's bloody vile and I've never hated someone so much in all my life. She's just got one of those faces that you just want to ram into a brick wall, but you just know it won't do enough damage that you want it to, you know?"

"What's her deal in all of this then?"

"Seriously, I wish I bloody knew. She's supposed to be Max's PA, yet I've never once seen her working while I've been over there. She just turns up whenever she feels like it for no apparent reason. In fact the only time I ever saw her there was when she was making my life hell, or taking advantage of a fragile situation and chose that moment to make a pass at Max."

"Nooo..." George shouts before his hand flys up and clamps over his mouth.

"I'm telling you, she's a fucking fruit cake and she sure as hell wouldn't last two minutes with Jen around. Actually, speaking of Jen, how is she? I haven't gotten around to calling her since I've been home yet."

"I reckon she'll be pretty made up to see you actually.

I think you've come back at just the right time." His face pales as he gives my arm a quick squeeze.

"What did you mean?" I ask, slightly confused. "What's happened? Is she okay?" George glances at his watch before standing and reaches out for my cup.

"I hate to do this princess, but I've gotta get back to work."

"George Matthews!" I shout. "You best tell me what's happened right now."

"It's really not my place to say. Just call her okay? You'll understand once you've spoken to her."

What the fuck. Surely nothing serious could have happened to her. I only spoke to her last week and she seemed absolutely fine. She's always the first to tell me if something's wrong.

I quickly stop in at Stanton's on my way back from lunch to let Tim know that I'm calling it a day, but I'll be available on the mobile. It shouldn't surprise me that Amelia's AWOL again. Something really needs sorting about that. You can't run a business with people who are happy and willing to take the piss constantly. One thing I am certain of is that it needs nipping in the bud, and fast. There is no way she would have acted like this while Mal was here and if Mal left Tim in charge, then she shouldn't be acting any different.

I can't get what George said out of my head. When I come to think of it, I've not actually heard from Jen since our last Skype session. Normally I'll get at least a few texts throughout the day about random shit, but I've had nothing. I quickly check my email to see if she's responded to the last email I sent her the other day but nada, nothing is there. Deciding to give her a call, I make my way to the tube. It's just as busy as I remember with everyone trying to get from A to B on their daily commute. One thing I haven't missed is the obscene amount of smelly armpits being shoved in my face. It's bloody horrid. People don't need to concern themselves with pepper spray, all they need is to be armed with a can of deodorant to fend of these people. They'll end up shrinking away like a witch does to water.

I arrive at Jens within half an hour and instantly I know that something is off. For a start her blinds are shut. The last time this happened, she'd completely closed herself off from the world while she overdosed on Ben and Jerry's and re-runs of friends when Alex, the then, love of her life decided that she no longer had the right tools for the job, much to George's amusement.
I haven't got a clue what's happened since I spoke to her last, but I swear to god if that knob has fucked her over, heads are going to roll.
"Jen... Jen it's me." I shout through the letter box. "Jen, bloody hell, I know you're in there. I can hear the tele." If she doesn't open this door in the next two minutes I'm going to boot it down. "Answer the fucking door Davies, right now!"
I hear the lock go and nothing can prepare me for the sight that is before me.
"Shit Jen." Her hair is in tatters and her mascara is all down her face from crying. She looks a right bloody mess. As if seeing me sets her off again and I pull her into my arms trying to reassure her that everything will be okay.
"Shhh, it's okay I'm here now." I soothe. I walk forwards with her still in my arms and lead her into the living room. I've never seen her look so broken and it tears me up inside.
"Jess I don't know what to do. How did I let it all get out of control?"
"How about I make us a brew and you can start from

the beginning? I'm not going anywhere in a hurry."
She doesn't answer me so I make my way to the kitchen. If this is down to Luke I'm going to fucking rip his balls off. I know she falls quickly, but to see her like this is unusual. It feels like it takes forever for the kettle to boil so while I wait I pull out my phone and message George.

I'm at Jens. What the hell has happened? She's a fucking mess and why did no one tell me about this?"

To say I'm pissed off is an understatement. Am I that much of a shit friend that no one has bothered to call me to tell me what's been happening? I thought George would have called me to tell me, seeing that he's obviously been in the know for some time.
I place Jen's mug in front of her as I sit on the couch beside her. She looks like a little child again, wrapped up in her blanket with tears streaming down her face.

"Why didn't you call me? I would have been back here in an instant." Stroking her hair, I wish I could make whatever was causing her pain to go away.

"Exactly. That's why I didn't call you. As much as I'd like you to, you wouldn't have been able to change anything anyway."

"Maybe not, but I would have been here for you and that's what's important. Is it Luke?" I ask unable to keep the question that has been dancing on my tongue back. The only answers I get are sniffles. "What's he done? Do I need to go all Jen on his arse, because I will do. I might not be a pro like you, but I'll bloody give it my best shot."

"He's not done anything wrong. Well not really. If I hadn't have been so stupid then none of this would have happened. What am I going to do Jess?"

"I'm not sure unless you tell me, love. If he's not upset you then what's gotten you in this state and don't say you're just hormonal because that's utter bullocks."

"Don't hate me, please." My heads mashed and I don't have a clue what she's saying. She is talking in bloody riddles. "

" could never hate you. Sure you get on my tits like I don't know what, but I could never, ever hate you." I continue to stroke her hair, anything to make her feel a little bit better. "Where's Luke now?"

"I don't know. I can't face him, every time he calls or try's to come around I feel physically sick. I can't even bring myself to message him back. Fucking hell, he probably thinks I'm such a bitch."

"But why? I don't get it. If he's not done anything wrong, then why would you ignore him?"

"I'm pregnant Jess."

I instantly burst out laughing and I can't help it. "Piss off Jen. Now isn't the time for pissing around." I wait for a smile to creep across her face to let me know she's trying to make light of a bad situation, but it doesn't come. Instead, she sits and looks at me with those puppy dog eyes and her bottom lip trembling as she tries to stop herself from crying again.

"You're being serious aren't you? How do you know? Are you late?"

"I've done ten tests, Jess and every single one of them is fucking positive."

"Shit. Have you been to the doctors?"

"I've not left the house since I found out. George got suspicious and called round and kind of put two and two together."

"And does Luke know?"

"Of course doesn't. What do you take me for? Me being so bloody careless has ruined everything for the both of us."

"You don't know that. Wait, does that test tell you how far you are?"

"No but I can only be about four weeks, max. I haven't slept with anyone else for months."

"I'm not saying that, you dopey cow. I'm just wondering how we're going to get you through this?"

"What do you mean?"

"Well first things first. You're not staying here on your own tonight. You go and get a bath, you smell pretty bad." I shrug, "When you get out, I'll make you something to eat and then tomorrow you'll be going to the doctors with me. They'll need to check you over and stuff."

Jess

"I can't believe you brought me here so that I'm surrounded by sick people. What if I catch something in my condition? How selfish are you? You're supposed to be my friend."

"Oh don't be such a wingebag. If you get ill then you'll just have to deal with it like everyone else does."

"You can be such a heartless cow at times you know." She says as she jabs me playfully in the ribs. It's good to see that she's got a bit of her personality back at least. "Thank you."

"What for?"

"For being here. It means a lot."

"Don't be daft, where else would I be you silly mare?" Honestly at times I wonder how she functions on her own. She's like a walking hazard.

"Miss Davies." After an hour long wait, we're finally called into the doctor's office and she instantly turns a delightful shade of green. If it wasn't such a sensitive issue for her, I'd whip out my phone and take a picture for the Jess and Jen adventure album. "What brings you to us today Miss Davies?" The doctor smiles encouragingly at her and I give her arm a light squeeze in encouragement.

"Um... I believe that I may be pregnant."

"Well congratulations. I take it that you have already done a test?" Jen doesn't say anything; she just nods her head in the doctor's direction, most likely desperate to get this over with.

"Okay well first things, first. Please could you fill this for me and come back in once you have done it." Jen's handed a piss pot and she doesn't look happy about it in the slightest.

"But I've already done a test."

"Of course, but policy states you have to do another one for your medical records and it will also allow me to check everything is how it should be."

She gets up on a huff and makes her way to the ladies while muttering something that sounds like *"this is so fucking embarrassing."* One of these days she'll do as she's told without moaning about it. When she returns she sheepishly hands the doctor her sample for her to test.

"Thank you." She says and after a few moments she looks at Jen. "Okay, well Miss Davies it would seem that you're not pregnant."

"That can't be possible, I did ten tests and they all came back positive."

"Could I ask which tests you used?"

"Erm, I don't remember the brand but I picked them up from the quid shop."

"Not all of those brands are accurate. Also it would seem that there have been quite a few recalls on some tests recently, as they have been giving out false readings. It would seem that you were unlucky to pick up some from the bad batch."

"I wouldn't call it unlucky. Shitting hell, I've spent a week in torture. I can't look after myself, let alone a baby." She squeals.

"Jen!" I hiss, trying to remind her where we are. Fortunately the doctor seems to understand her predicament.

"If you haven't had a period in the next two weeks or so, then I'd like you to come back to see me so that we can run some more tests. I'd just like to make sure everything is working how it should be. Oh and you have also missed your routine smear. As soon as we have this issue resolved I'd like you to book into have that done too."

"I can't tell you how shitting happy I am right now Jess. I literally feel like I could piss rainbows." I look at my best friend and feel a sudden wave of relief wash over me.

"Me too. You wouldn't be able to cope with a baby, Jen. You're far too high maintenance yourself. So are you going to call Luke now?"

"I guess I better do soon. What am I going to say to him? He's going to think I'm such a bitch for ignoring him."

"The fact that he kept trying to contact you shows he's still in to you. Just tell him you were I'll with the flu or something."

"And this is why I love you. You always know what to do."

"I have my moments, love. Maybe it's about time you got yourself on the pill so we don't have another repeat of the past twenty four hours. What do you say?"

"My two favourite ladies. What can I get for you?"

"The usual and something greasy for this deprived one." I say signaling to Jen who graces him with a beaming smile.

"It's good to see you back to your usual self."

"Well this one dragged me to the doctors this morning and it's was only a bloody false alarm, wasn't it? How about we celebrate? I can feel nine months' worth of shots in my foreseeable future."

"I'll bring them over so we can get planning."

Max

I've been sat outside Jess' house for an hour and her fucking phone is switched off. AGAIN. I've tried Stanton's and the place is closed for the day. What the fuck is going on. I'll give her another half an hour and then I'll head to Luke's if she doesn't show. I didn't think to call her to let her know I was flying out and I don't know if she's spoken to Liss. All I want to do is see her beautiful face and then curl up into her body as I sleep for a week. Fucking jet lag. How she's even up and about I'll never know. Maybe I should have called at Jens. Why didn't I think of calling there sooner? Of course that's where she'll be. Those two are inseparable. I stick my car into drive and make my way down the street eager to see her. I'm still fucking pissed that she went when I told her not to, but that's Jess, always ready to do the opposite of what I fucking ask of her.

I'm only parked up for about ten minutes when I see her bouncy honey waves coming towards the house. Fuck how I've missed her. She's fucking perfect. I decide against calling out to her to see if she notices me. Instead it's Jen that comes barreling over towards the car.

"Hey muscles. I didn't expect to see you here, that's for sure."

"Yeah? I'm full of surprises, me." I say smiling at her.

"Max?" Jess chimes in. Shock registers all over her face followed by disbelief that I'm actually here. "What are you doing here?" She asks.

"I came to help out at Stanton's and to personally show you what happens when you fuck off without telling me, angel." She leans in towards the car window.

"Oh, kinky. I like this one, Jess. Do whatever you have to do to keep him, because I'm telling you, if I get my hands on him I ain't ever giving him back."

"Piss off." She says jokingly but if push came to shove I can see it in her eyes that she'd be pissed as hell. "When did you get here? Why didn't you call?"

"A few hours back." I could say so much more seeing as she did the same, but for now I leave it as I get out of the car. Without a moment's notice I pull her into me and press my lips to hers. "Don't you dare fucking leave me again, lady."

"I didn't leave you. I was always coming back?" Part of me always hoped that would be the answer, but it still feels fucking good to hear it come from those beautiful lips.

"I'd fly anywhere to be with you."

"Come on you two, you'll get arrested with that show of PDA."

I stay at Jen's for a while with Jess firmly positioned in between my legs on the sofa. She's been away from me for far too long and I don't plan on letting go of her anytime soon, unless I have too.

"Where's Luke? I thought he'd be here. You two were pretty much inseparable last time I saw you both."

"Erm, yeah I've had a bit of man flu and wanted to protect the balls that he doesn't have. I'm kind like that you see. He'll probably be around later." She shrugs. "Oh, you're a sneaky one muscles. You haven't even told him you're here yet, have you?"
Jess' phone chimes to life beside us, and she quickly reaches to grab it before it rings off. "Like I said, I'm full

of surprises."

"Hi. Yeah, no it's fine honestly. What? Really? At least it's a start." Jess says with a glum luck on her face. "Did they give you a name of the client that been affected? Okay... Yep, that's one of the biggies."

She turns to look at me as she ends the call, desperate to tell me something.

"I knew it was a hacking, I just bloody knew it. It's one of our biggest clients too, Limitless."

"Limitless isn't just the biggest client, Jess. That's mine and Mal's company files with every aspect of personal information on there. It's the company that's been targeted, not a client."

"Are you sure? It can't be. Tim said that the client knew and they were threatening legal action. It just doesn't make sense."

"You've fucking got that right, angel. Listen I'm gonna head to Stanton's to see if I can get to the bottom of this, but I'll see you back at yours later, okay?"

"Hmm mmm." She nods as I lean in for a kiss and she hands me the keys. Something dodgy is going down and I'm going to find out exactly what it is.

The office is eerily quiet as I open the door. Why the fuck is Stanton's closed? Surely there's more staff than Jess as Tim?

"Hey, yeah it's Max." I say answering the phone. "I need your help on something. One of my servers has been hacked and I need to know who's responsible. I'd like to think it's not an inside job, but I need to be sure. Get me the dates, location and all that shit and call me back as soon as you have it. Make it fucking quick."

I won't stand for anyone trying to fuck up my family business. Mal's worked too hard to build this up to where it is today, and I won't allow anyone to destroy it. I take a quick look over the accounts while I wait on

Heath getting back to me. Everything else seems to be fine; it's just the limitless file. Not only does it have the business details on there and upcoming proposals that me and Mal have put together, but all staff details and pay role information. If this gets into the wrong hands, we're in big shit.

Jess

"Why does he have to be so goddamn hot, woman? I hope you realise how lucky you are."

"Oh yes, yes I do." I smile knowing that yes, I really am.

"You've got Luke, he's pretty hot too, you know."

"Yeah, that's if he doesn't think I'm some super psycho bitch after the way I have been acting towards him."

"Come on Jen. This is you that we're taking about. Of course he knows you're psycho. It's one of your many charms."

"Oh piss off, you bitch. I had a bloody good reason for my actions and you know it." She laughs.

"Well to be fair, if you would have used something then you wouldn't have found yourself in that situation would you?" A cushion is suddenly hurled at me from her direction.

"Quit being a fucking bitch. I've learnt my lesson okay?"

"Oh yeah, I meant to ask earlier, have you seen or heard from Amelia since I've been away?" Her absence is still playing on my mind.

"Not that I can remember, why?"

"It's just that she's been AWOL from work quite a lot and no one can get hold of her. She's basically just going about doing what she wants from what Tim's said."

"Maybe she just needs sometime out, or something. She wasn't well just before you left was she?"

A knock sounds at the door and Jen turns to look at me with utter panic in her eyes. "Oh god, that's going to be Luke. Shit Jess, what do I say?"

"Just be yourself and you'll be fine."

"Shit, shit, shit. I can't do this."

"You can, and you bloody well will. Just think of the conversation that you would have been having if there was a mini diva growing inside of you." She shudders at my words and I can't help but laugh. "My point exactly now quit being so soft."

When it becomes apparent that she's going nowhere fast, and the knocks continue to get louder and louder, I pull myself up from the sofa on a dramatic sigh and look at her. "Grow yourself a fucking pair Davies." I mutter as I walk towards the front door.

I stand in shock at the person stood before me on the opposite side of the threshold. Anger, sadness and panic all set in and my hands start to shake.

"What are you doing here?" I ask.

"Is that really all you have to say to me after all this time?"

"What do you expect me to say?" I ask and my words come out on a choke as I fight back the tears that threaten to fall.

"Jess, who is it?" Jens voice flows through from the living area.

"How did you know where I was?" I ask, completely ignoring Jen's question.

"Josh. Who do you think? I'm glad he finally saw sense before you darkened his soul too, with your selfish ways."

I can't believe I'm hearing the words that are coming out of her mouth. It's one thing to have to listen to them over the phone, but dealing with them face to face is something else entirely.

"I'm not surprised he finally left you. It's about time he made something of himself, instead of you holding him back while you pretend to be something that you're not."

"I don't need to listen to your bullshit, mother. Maybe once you've sobered up a little I might be prepared to talk to you civilly. Can't you see that you need help?"

"It's a pleasure as always Diana." Jen says with venom in her voice as she sneaks up behind me. She must have heard the commotion from the living area and came to investigate. "You've caused enough damage in the past and I won't stand here and let you tear chunks out of Jess again, just so you can feel better about yourself. If you want to talk to Jess properly then you'll do it with a clear head. If you're not prepared to do that, then you can turn back around and walk back to wherever it was that you've come from."

"I'm surprised to see that you're still standing by Jess's side. Most people would have given up on her by now. Surely there are better people you can spend your time with Jennifer?"

The woman stood before me is pure evil. She is no mother, at least not when she's fueled with alcohol. She needs help and I wish that she could see it. It pains me like hell to see her like this, but I can't cope with the abuse she hurls at me. I swear to god, I'm going to kill Josh when I get my fucking hands on him for giving out Jens address.

"Alright, now you've had your say. Why don't you do what Jess says and come back once you've sobered up some?"

My mother changes instantly at Jens words. No longer is she the sour faced woman that I have come to know, instead, she now begins to slide down Jens doorframe with her head in her hands. As she pulls them away slightly, I see that she's actually crying.

"Why don't you love me Jess?" She shouts. "Why don't you care? Why don't you need me like you're supposed to?" I have no words, no words to say how I feel as I watch my mum, the one person who was supposed to protect me from harm and protect me no matter what; crumble and breakdown before my own eyes. Instead, all I can do is watch as Jen takes over. Bending down, she slowly removes my mother's worn and battered hands away from her face.

"Diana, I need you to listen to me. You need to get some help. As much as you're suffering and hurting, you can't keep taking it out on Jess, because in turn you're hurting her just as much, if not more. You lashing out at her every time you've had a drink isn't doing either of you any good."

"I've... Got... Nowhere... To... Go." She splutters between each breath. "I've lost everything Jess. The house, the car, it's all gone."

Everything around me feels as though it's collapsing and my lungs struggle to take in air as I take in her words.

"You can't leave her with nothing Jess." Jen looks at me pleadingly to say something. I'm tempted to turn around and go back inside. Maybe then she'll see how reckless she's been when she actually realises what she's done.

"Come on Di, how about we try and sober you up first? One line out of turn mind and you're out, understand?" Jen asks but by the time my mums head has hit the pillow she's out like a light.

"Bloody hell Jess. I knew she was bad, but not *that* bad. She needs help.

"You're telling me." I say as I look over at my mum and can't help but notice how much she's aged since I saw her last. She's barely recognizable as she sleeps.

"What am I going to do? I've got to sort all this shit out at Stanton's. Yesterday, I thought you were going to be pushing out a mini diva and now my mums bloody homeless. I never thought I'd say this Jen, but I'm beginning to regret coming back home already."

Dealing with the queen bitch is actually more bearable than this.

"Well, she can stay here tonight. I know you're not comfortable with her staying at yours. You know I won't tolerate her bullshit, either and I'll even feed her too for you. I'm good at looking after people."

"Don't be daft. She can't stay here, plus she's my responsibility, so I'll just deal with the situation one way or another. I'll stick around until she wakes up. Thanks though."

After three long hours my mum finally resurfaces from her slumber."Nice of you to finally join us." I say, my tone still icy.

"I'll fix us a coffee." Jen chimes in and I smile at her in thanks. I look over to my mum and wonder where it all went wrong so fast.

"What's happened mum? How did you manage to lose the house?" She rubs her hands down her face. Whether it's from shame or her banging head I can't be sure. Either way, it's bloody self-inflicted. One thing is certain; she isn't leaving here until I find out exactly what's happened and why.

"I lost my job."

"What do you mean you lost your job?" It's going from bad to bloody worse every time she talks. My mum may be many things, but work shy isn't one of them. She has always prided herself on working and she's always loved a challenge. She bloody loved her job. I think that's the only thing that she passed on to me.

"When?" I demand.

"About six months ago, everything got on top of me. Well more than usual anyway and I thought what's the point? *You* weren't around anymore and no one else bothered with me, I can't tell you how long I would go without someone picking up the phone to call me, only for it to be those bloody telesales pestering about this and that. I've been alone for a long time Jess, especially here." She holds her hand to her chest and I can't stop mine from tightening in response. "I just couldn't handle it anymore. One day I called in sick and that day rolled into a week, which then turned into a month and so on. Before I knew it, everything around me was hazed with a big dark cloud and I couldn't face going out of the house for more than fifteen or so minutes at a time. If people didn't want to bother with me, why should I bother with them?"

"Why didn't you tell me this instead of hurling a shit load of abuse at me?" I ask.

"What do you care?" She snarls at me. "You had your own perfect fucking life to lead and god forbid your waste of a space mother would come and tarnish it. Why am I even telling you this anyway?"

That comment right there, instantly gets my back up and I have to bite back the retort that I want throw at her.

"Of course I care. No matter what happens you're still my mum. It's unfortunate that things have turned out the way they have between us, but I would never, never see you go without. Like anything, we'll get you through it;but first you need help mum. The first step is admitting you have a problem and then maybe we might just be able to get your life back on track. One thing I will say mum, is that if you continue being nasty to me, or blame me for dad leaving from this point on, then you're doing this on your own. This time I will walk out of your life for good and I'm being deadly serious. It isn't fair how you treat or speak to people."

"Here we are. Biscuits anyone?" Jen smiles and I raise my eyebrows at her. Only Jen could act like we're due to have royalty around while she's entertaining my pissed up mother.

Max

I've been fucking sat here waiting for Heath to call me back all afternoon and I'm starting to get pretty pissed, and fast. I've not slept for almost two days and I need this shit sorting ASAP. I've been in England for six hours and I've only managed to see Jess for half an hour. What the fucks that about?

I'm just about to call Heath, when my phone starts dancing to life in front of me.

"Hey." I hope he has some answers for me. If anyone's good for the job, then it's Heath.

"Hey mate. I got back to you as soon as I could. This shits been a hell of a lot trickier than we initially expected."

"What do you mean?" I ask, unsure if I actually want to know the answer from the tone in his voice.

"Well, we've located the file at least, and found which server hacked into it. You ain't gonna like what I'm about to tell you, Max. It's likely going to take a whole lot of digging to find out exactly who's responsible for it, but you should be good for that. The one thing that's worrying me is that the location where the file was removed from was in your office, not Stanton's."

"You sure?" There's no fucking way my own security details could have been hacked in my own office. No one has access to those drives but me and Jess and she sure as hell doesn't have the password to crack it.

"I'm telling you clear as day, mate. The host and IP address is exactly the same to the one in Jess' office. I checked it out myself to be sure. If you give me the go ahead, I'll get the whole computer checked to see what's on there."

"Sure, do whatever you have to do and come back to me ASAP."

This shits getting fucked up? Why would that data be on Jess' computer? There's no way that she'd need to access it, let alone take it. Nothing seems to be adding up and who the hell is this so called *client* threatening legal action? The only client of Limitless is Mal and I, and neither of us are demanding or threatening anything. I need to try and find out where that call came from and who's been throwing out these demands.

I try to call Jess again before I set off, but her phones still switched off. That woman needs to learn that a phone is to be used. I doubt that she's eaten and I'm fucking starving so I stop off at the local Chinese and grab us a bite to eat. I've been looking forward to winding down with her all pissing day and if we're lucky we'll get no interruptions for a long while.

The lights are on low as I pull up outside Jess' house, so it's a pretty good sign that she's still awake. I get out and knock on, unsure if she's actually expecting me. When the door opens, a woman who I have never seen before stands in front of me.

"Is Jess around?" I ask, not sure if I like the way this woman's looking at me.

"Who's asking?" The look she gives me is one of utter dislike. "What do you want with her?"

What the fuck? "Can you tell her it's Max?"

"Mum, who is it? Oh hey Max, I meant to call you earlier."

"No worries. I wasn't sure if you'd eaten so I thought I'd grab you something on my way back." I lean in to hand over to bag much to this woman's utter distaste.

"I'll come back tomorrow."

"No, no. Don't be silly, that's not what I meant." The smile that lights up her eyes instantly tells me that she's glad to see me. Her posture however is telling me that she's holding something back. The woman begrudgingly steps to the side to let me pass. Jess looks at me apologetically as I walk by her.

"Excuse my mother. She can be a little standoffish to people that she doesn't know."

"A little?" Jeez if she could get away with harming me I'm sure she would have done it on first sight.

"Well Jessica. Are you going to tell me who this *delightful* looking man is that's turned up out of the blue to feed you?"

"Give over mum. What did I say about being nasty to people? This is Max. He's umm, a work colleague. Max meet my mum."

Well this definitely isn't how I expected *meet the parents* to go down. I feel better knowing that I didn't actually lie to Mal when I told him Jess had to see her mum. I just hope after an hour or so, she's warmed more towards me.

"Did you manage to get everything sorted at the office?"

"Kind off. A few issues have come from the investigations that Heath carried out, but nothing we need to worry about." I hate twisting the truth when it comes to Jess, but I'm not sure what to say until Heath has looked into it further, plus her mums watching me like a hawk. She fucking looks at me like I've got too heads.

"You seem pretty happy to be back." The glow in her face is evident and it looks so fucking good on her.

"I had a really good catch up with Jen and I think I needed it. We don't function that well when we're separated."

"Yeah? I never would have guessed. So Mrs Townsend, can I call you Mrs Townsend?"

"Diana will do." She snaps at me and Jess shoots her a warning glance.

"Well it's a pleasure to meet you Diana. Do you live locally?" I try to start a conversation to let her know I'm not the bad guy, but Jess jumps in and stops me.

"Hey mum. I'm going to call it a night. I'm still shattered from the flight back and I bet you could do with some sleep too?"

"Now that you mention it, I'm pretty beat." I say as I stand, ready to grab my keys.

"Max, wait a minute." She turns back to her mum and says, "I've laid out some stuff for you in the spare room. If you need anything help yourself okay? And I expect you to still be here when I get up in the morning."

Jess

I leave my mum in the front room once I'm sure she knows where everything is and make my way over to the man that I have been desperate to see for days. The stolen moments that I've managed to spend with him today have been few and far between and as much as I'd never admit it to him, I've missed him like mad.

"You're not going are you?" I ask, suddenly panicking on the inside that I'm going to have to go another night without him by my side.

"Yeah. I was going to head to Luke's and crash there for a bit. I'll come by first thing in the morning and take you for breakfast without a certain someone eyeing me like a hawk."

"Yeah, I'm so sorry about my mum. Seriously she's a nightmare at the best of times, but she's in a bad place at the minute. Still it doesn't excuse her attitude towards you in the slightest."

"Don't worry about it, angel. I've experienced much worse." He says and his hand automatically reaches out, grabbing my hip and pulling me in close to him.

"I've missed you so fucking much angel."

"Don't go then. Stay here with me.It's pointless going back out, plus you don't even know if he'll be home."

"You sure?"

"Hmm mm. Of course I'm sure. Thanks for dinner too. Food completely skipped my mind after the day I've had today."

"That bad huh? How about I try and make it end a little better for you?"

"Now that sounds promising, but I'd hate to dent your ego and fall asleep mid action. That's how tired I am."

"Angel, it's not possible for you to fall asleep while I'm buried deep inside of you, believe me." As he leans into kiss me, I'm scooped up into his big strong arms as he carries me up the stairs.

As I'm brushing my teeth, I watch Max's reflection through the mirror and I openly perv on him as he removes his clothing. The muscles in his back tense and flex as he lifts and stretches and he looks like an absolute Adonis. I still can't believe that he's here with me. Shit, I still can't get over the fact that he actually followed me all this way. He's pretty fucking special. My eyes stay trained on him as he makes his way over to me. His arms snake around my hips as he presses himself against me and his touch sends trails of fire dancing across my body.

"I'm still pissed that you flew out when I told you not too." His face is serious in the reflection, but his tone is playful.

"Really? Max I'm an adult and I make my own decisions. Surely you should know this by now? If not, you're in a for a pretty big shock pal." I tease and wriggle my arse into him. I'm greeted with a satisfied groan.

As soon as I have finished cleaning myself up, I'm spun around into his arms and his mouth is on mine in seconds. Claiming exactly what he wants, when he wants. The taste and feel of his body pressed against mine works me up into a bloody frenzy.

"I've missed this." He's says as he pulls me in closer to him. "These past few weeks have been fucking torture, Jess. Do you know what you do to me?" Oh yes I do. I do indeed."You're lucky I'm not punishing you for disrespecting my wishes, lady."

I'm not sure how I fell about that. Threatened by the seriousness of his tone or turned on from the unknown.

"Maybe I'll have to disobey you more often Mr Wild, so that I can find out exactly what that entails." I lift up onto my tip toes and kiss him briefly on the nose. "But for now, I really, really need to go to sleep."

I wake up suddenly and the room is still dark. A faint moan escapes from Max's lips and I turn to lean in to him just to make sure he's really here. The moment my hands reach out to touch him he cries out in what I can only describe as agony.

"Get the fuck of me. Don't you dare fucking touch me."

"What?" I recoil against his harsh words and feel the tears begin to fill my eyes.

"No. Fucking stay away from me." He shouts and then the bed stats to rock. It's then that I realise he isn't really talking to me. He must be talking in his sleep.

"Max, shhh it's okay." I try to soothe him, but my voice just triggers him off even more.

"I said get your fucking hands off her. Jess, no please." I jump up and switch the light on to see that he's rigid in the bed and his hands are gripping the sheets so tight that his hands have gone white. Shit what do I do? Do I try to wake him up or will that just make him worse? I've never experienced anything like this before. Worried he might lash out in his sleep, I pick up one of the scatter cushions and toss it at his head. He doesn't wake, but he loosens his grip on the sheet a little. He still breathes out small little moans as he turns back on to his side. I remain seated on my chair until his ragged breathing seems to have calmed down.

"What you doing over there, angel?" I look up and

see that his eyes are now open, concern etched all around them. "You having trouble sleeping?"

"Are you okay?" I ask deciding to get back into bed.

"I am now that I know you're still here with me."

"You we're having some kind of nightmare, I think." Max sits up instantly at my words and rubs both of his hands through his hair. He looks so fucking beautiful no matter what time of day.

"Shit. Jess I'm sorry. I didn't hurt you did I? Please tell me I didn't hurt you." He looks at me intently searching my face for any sign that he did.

"No, no of course you didn't hurt me, but you seemed like you were in pain yourself."

"I didn't mean to scare you angel. Come here." I get up and lean into the comfort of his open arms and rest my head against his warm chest. At least his breathing seems to be back under control. "I'd never hurt you angel. I'd rather die than allow anyone to hurt you." He says those words with such a passion, that I don't think for a second that he's lying.

My mum is already up and dressed by the time we get downstairs. There's a fresh pot of coffee on the counter top with two mugs waiting for us. I look over at her as if to say *what the hell?*

"My way of saying thanks for yesterday."
I smile at my mum and I'm thankful for the first time in god knows how many years that she has been more than civil towards me first thing in the morning.

"Diana." Max says as he follows behind me. I don't know what my mum's problem is with him. Whenever I look at Max, all I see is my loveable rogue with his messy hair, piercing blue eyes and day old stubble and think he's the most perfect thing I have ever had the pleasure of laying my eyes on. My mother probably just sees the rogue side. I walk over to the counter to pour myself and Max a coffee, and instantly feel him behind me.

"You luck so fucking beautiful when you wake up, you know? It's a shame your mothers here otherwise we'd have other, more exciting things to take care of." He leans in closer to me and nibbles my ear and my body goes weak at the contact. That fucking man. Why is he doing this to me? It's fucking torture.

"Baby steps remember?" I say and a wicked grin graces his lips as he makes his way over to the table.

"What do you have planned today, Jessica?" I look at my mother, a little taken aback by her question. She never, ever asks me about my plans. I guess I should take her new personality with a pinch of salt, because I doubt it will last for long.

"I've got a few loose ends to tie up at Stanton's and then I'll head to the shops to get some food in. What about you?"

'I'm thinking it's about time I got out of your hair. You don't need me here cramping your style, do you? I'll pop down to the letting agents and see what they have available."

I instantly place my cup down on the table and look her sternly in the eye. "Mum, you know it's not as easy as that. You can stay here until you get back on your feet. There's no rush for you to go anywhere, as long as you quit it with the attitude. Who knows, maybe this is what we both need? Maybe we could try and start again?"

Max clears his throat and I'm suddenly brought back to the here and now. Shit. I hope he hasn't picked up on anything.

"I've got some stuff to go over with Heath, so I'll leave you ladies to it. Call me later and let me know what you're doing?"

"Hmm mm." I nod and lean into him for a goodbye

kiss. "See you later."

"Oh Jess?"

"Yes?"

"Do me a favour and charge your phone. It's a bloody nightmare trying to get hold of you at the best of times."

I watch him leave and I'm fully aware that I have the biggest dopey arse smile on my face.

"He's going to rip your heart out girl." My mother pipes up as I sit back down. "They're all the same. Men like that only want one thing. A bloody good time, until they find someone else."

"Mum, we're not serious; we're just seeing how things go right now."

"That's what I said with your dad and look how that turned out. Your dad turned heads wherever he went. Everyone knew him and everyone wanted him. I'll never forget how he made me feel. I was instantly attracted to him but I kept my distance for some time. All I ever heard was *Di, don't do it. He's going to break your heart and you'll never be able to fix it*." She looks off into the distance and I don't know what to say. I've never heard my mum talk about my dad like this before.
Normally she's closed off and never speaks about him unless she's slagging him off for one thing, or another. "He never stopped pursuing me though. He'd wow me with flowers and spontaneous visits at work, until one day I eventually gave in. I let him take me on a date and it was the best date a girl could ever wish for."

"What did you do?" I ask, intrigued at the story of my mums past.

"Well I finally said yes and on the day I stuck my glad rags on and waited for him to collect me. He was early, which surprised me and he took me to a fast food diner, where we happily ate burgers and drank milkshake." She smiles while in thought and it's so good to see. "It was one of the happiest days of my life."

"It sounds like you had a blast."

"Oh we did. You see, I know that's how you're feeling right now, ecstatic in your perfect little bubble of happiness, I was the same. This Max, sure he might be a decent guy, but he reminds me of your father too much for me to take to him just yet. His arrogance, his persona, it's all the same. Just watch your heart with him Jess, because if you are anything like me at all; you won't recover from the damage. Look at me after all these years, I'm still trying to figure out how."

"Like I said earlier, you can stay here for as long as you need to. Get yourself on the right track, get a job and then we can look at getting you a new place, okay?"

"I've never said this often enough Jessica. Thank you and I'm sorry for the way I have treated you in the past."

"Don't worry about it, like you said, it's in the past. As long as it stays there, then we can both move on and try and make something of this relationship."

I leave my mum back at mine while I pop out to check how things are going on at Stanton's. Hopefully Max has managed to find out some more information from Heath so we can try and sort this mess out before Mal gets wind of it. The tube's packed as usual, and today I remembered to wrap up warm to protect myself from the icy gale. How I took my leisurely walks along the beach for granted.

Soon enough I'm rocking up to Joe's with numb hands, a tad windswept and a delightful red nose. Oh how attractive I must look to all the passers-by.

"Can I get two flat whites and a cappuccino from the hot barrister, please?" I say with a smile as I try to fight off the clatter of my teeth.

"How's your mum?" George asks while he works his magic. "Gotta say princess, it came as a bit of a shock to find out that she's staying at yours."

"Tell me about it. I woke up this morning and it took me a moment to remember that she was there, but I can't leave her homeless can I?"

"You can if she starts giving you shit again. I hope she realises how lucky she is that you've taken her in."

"Don't worry, I've already had a talk with her. She's officially been warned. Any funny business and she'll be out on her ear."

"I believe that the sex god is also back on English turf, too?" I can't hide the smile that lights up my face at the mention of Max's name?

"Yes he is. I've not seen him as much as I would have liked, to be honest. I'm not going to lie, I'm getting desperate to spend some alone time with him but it just isn't happening."

"Princess. If that was me, he wouldn't have left my bedroom. A man like that is to be used purely for your enjoyment." I laugh as an elderly woman gasps in shock beside me. Bloody George, he has no shame, no matter where he is, and I love him for it. He leans over the bar, much to the woman's distaste and gives me a peck on the cheek before passing me my drinks.

"See you later, tiger" I say and wink at him. If you can't beat 'em, join 'em and all that. It feels so good to have my friends around me again, but for how long, I can't be sure.

"I come bearing gifts." I shout as I walk into Stanton's. It should come as no surprise to see Max seated in Mal's office looking sexy as hell with his tie loose around his neck, top button open and his sleeves bunched up at the elbows. Damn he is utter perfection. He catches me biting down on my bottom lip, while I check him out and he greets me with that devilishly wicked grin of his and I blush instantly.

"Oh is that coffee?" Tim asks as I step further into the office.

"You bet'cha." I look around to see if Amelia has made an appearance, but surprise, surprise; she isn't here. I really need to remember to try and call her again later.

"Any news on Heath?" I ask Max as I pass him his flat white.

"Not yet, but hopefully soon. Hey, I've been thinking things over with this. Did you see anyone in the office or hanging about looking suspicious when I wasn't around?"

"No. That's impossible isn't it? I thought only us two and the PA's had access to that floor?"

"It is, or at least it should be. Have you noticed anything strange going on here recently, Tom?"

"It's Tim." I nudge him in the ribs with my elbow as he smiles playfully and pulls me down into his lap. Oh how I love playful Max.

"Not that I've noticed. There's only been me here most of the time anyway, to tell you the truth mate."

"Why? Do you think this was done deliberately by someone we know, trust even?"

"I'm not too sure, but I'll try my goddamed hardest to find out. That phone call you received Tim, do you remember if it was male of female?"

"Oh yes I remember. The caller was definitely female. That's what got my suspicions on high alert as I thought she might have been a reporter or something trying to dig for dirt. That's when I knew I needed to call Jess."

"Did she have an accent at all...?" Max asks, but cuts off all of a sudden when a commotion breaks out in reception.

"Why are you following me? Do you not listen? I told you to fuck off." I hear Amelia's voice before I step out of the office. What's happened now? Another row with the boyfriend? Well at least she's here. She still has her back to me as she continues to hurl insults to whoever it is that's following her.

"You can't do this to me. How the fuck could you have been so stupid? You do realise that you've ruined everything that I ever had don't you."

I freeze instantly on the spot as I hear that all too familiar voice. This can't be happening. It's all got to be one fucked up dream.

"Excuse me?" She shouts unaware of the audience she now has behind her. "Don't you dare blame me for this. Just because you weren't getting any at home and needed to stick it elsewhere."

"I'm warning you Amelia. Do not push me on this, you know how I feel about it. There's no way you can possibly go through with it."

"Just sit back and pissing watch me, you arsehole."

"How deluded can you be? Do you really think I'm going to father a child with a pyscho bitch like you?"

Everything suddenly turns into slow motion. I couldn't possibly have heard that right. A noise of some sort must escape me, because Josh suddenly turns to face me as I stand outside Mal's door with my mouth hanging wide open. Amelia notices a change is his face and turns to see what's suddenly caught his attention and when she sees me, she pales instantly.

After what feels like forever, I finally manage to speak. "You're pregnant? With him?" I whisper pointing my finger in Josh's direction. Oh my god I feel sick, I'm actually going to be sick right in front of everyone.

"Jess..." Josh says as he starts to walk towards me, but Max suddenly stands by my side and he stops in his tracks instantly.

"When? How do you two even know each other?" I begin and then suddenly everything clicks into place. "How could I have been so fucking stupid? You're *Mike?* All this time and I have been worried about some arsehole that's been upsetting you, and all along it was *him.* How long have you two been laughing at me. Fuck, I bet you've been having a whale of a time at my expense."

Amelia holds her hands up and steps towards me. "Jess I didn't know..."

"Don't." I cut her off. "You better thank your lucky fucking stars that you're pregnant, and you." I turn on Josh. "You can go and play with traffic, you twat."

I feel Max move closer to me, but it's taking everything I have not to break down and cry in front of everyone. How could they do this to me?

Max

I try to hold her, let her know that I am here, but she quickly storms out of the office without a backwards glance. It's pointless trying to stop her. Nothing I say now is going to make her feel any better. All I can do is be there for her when she needs me, and I'll fucking make sure that she doesn't need anyone else for the rest of her life.

With my fists clenched at my sides and my jaw working overtime, I look at the self-centred prick stood before me and all I want do is rip his fucking throat out. I didn't like him the first time I saw him, and I sure as hell don't like him any better now.

"I think it's best that you leave while you still can." He looks at me as if noticing me for the first time since he arrived here.

"This has got fuck all to do with you pal so how about you back the fuck off to where you came from?"

"That's where you're wrong. It's got every goddamn fucking thing to do with me. You might have hurt and fucked her over in the past, but I sure as hell won't stand back and watch you hurt her again. I'll give you one more chance, which is more than what you deserve. You either leave now while you still can, or I'll personally make sure that you won't be using your legs, or anything else for that matter, for a very fucking long time, *pal.* Am I making myself clear yet? And you," I look at Amelia, Jess' so called friend in utter disgust. "I'll see you in my office. Now!" I order.

Josh doesn't wait around for long. The little prick

shouldn't even be able to father a child the ball less bastard.

"Don't even think about contacting her either." I growl after him.

"Take a seat." I signal to the chair opposite me and wait for Amelia to sit down. She's gone a perfect shade of green and I don't know if that's the crazy hormones that women have when they're pregnant, or if she's actually sickened at what she's done. Either way, at this moment in time I couldn't give a toss.

"I just want to apologise for my outburst. It was completely unprofessional and it won't happen again." She says, practically on the verge of tears.

"You bet it won't. I don't think it's me that you need to be apologising to either, do you? That's not the reason why I called you in here. I think it's about time we had a little chat about your absent and lateness issues."

"I've had a couple of days..."

"That's to be expected given your, erm, situation. However every business has a policy in place for sickness and so on, and it needs to be followed at all times. The first being that you contact your employer to let them know if you won't be coming into work. I'm not sure how Mal deals with his HR stuff, but I've had a look at your file and you've never been absent while he's been here."

"I tried to call, numerous times but no one picked up."

"There are other methods that you could have used, Amelia. You have Tim's mobile or the works email address, right? Being AWOL is gross misconduct and a sackable offence."

"You're firing me? Does Mal even know about this?"

"Not yet ,and no he doesn't, but I can promise you that if he knew how you had been treating your job, he most likely would have fired you ages ago. I understand that you're not well at the moment and you've got some personal issues going on, so what I suggest is that you take some time out. I think it's unwise that you and Jess should be working together at the minute, don't you?"

She looks at me and mouths a silent "Thank you." to me.

"Don't thank me. I'm not doing this for my benefit. Between me and you, if you weren't pregnant, then I would have fired you, but fortunately for you the ball isn't in my court. That power right now lies with Jess. Go home and think about what you want and how seriously you take this job."

She stands to leave, but pauses as if she wants to say something to me but thinks better of it.

"We'll be in touch soon. Oh, and Amelia, keep Josh away from Stanton's. I won't have another scene like that in here, because next time I won't be so lenient."

My blood is pounding as she leaves and all I want to do is get to Jess. I have no idea where she is and her bloody phone isn't on again.

"Tim." I call out. "I'm going to see if I can find Jess. Will you be okay here?"

"Sure. Let her know I'm here if she needs me."

"I will." I pat him on the back, thankful that at least one of her colleagues is still looking out for her. I have no idea where she will be. Jens at work as I remember her saying something this morning about catching up with her tonight and I doubt she would have gone home with her mum there. The impression that I'm getting is that they're not the closest mother and daughter in the world. The only other place I can think of is the coffee house where George works. I hope to god I'm right. I could be out looking for her for hours, otherwise. The look on her face as she witnessed what those dicks had done back at Stanton's is still imprinted in my mind.

How I refrained from snapping that twats neck, is beyond me. He had a lucky escape, but if I see him anytime soon I can't guarantee that he'll have the same outcome.

I spot George as soon as I enter Joe's and he tilts his head towards the alcoves next to the window. My perfect angel looks completely lifeless as she sits with her legs curled beneath her and an extra-large coffee cup in her hands.

"Hey." I whisper as I approach, worried that if I speak any louder then I'll break what's left of her. She lifts her head up and she looks at me, her eyes swollen from crying a stream of constant tears and her cheeks all blotchy from where she must have been rubbing them. I want to reach out and make it all better, fuck I want to erase the whole goddamn day and erase what those two spineless pricks have done to my baby, but I can't. Instead I crouch down before her and cup her face between my hands.

"I'm so sorry angel."

"Don't you dare apologise for something that isn't your fault. I should have seen it coming a mile off. How could I have been so stupid Max? I feel like a fucking laughing stock."

Jess

Having Max beside me makes it a bit more bearable, but I'm still struggling to breathe. Every time I try to get a lung full of air my chest fights against me. I've been sat at Joe's for god knows how long, with my mind full of questions that won't go away. Ones that I can't face, or prepare myself to get the answers to. George has been amazing, giving me time to myself while keeping me in a warm supply of fresh coffee. It took me a while to stop him from marching out of here to confront Josh, but in the end I think he could see he was causing me more pain. I don't even want to think about Jens reaction. This time I reckon she will definitely try to rip his balls off.

Max lifts me up and positions me in his lap once he sits back down. I lean into him really close, worried that if I don't, he'll up and disappear out of my life and then I'll be left on my own. I don't want to think about being alone right now. I just want to sit like this, feeling the heat of Max beneath me, while he silently soothes me by stroking my hair; all while asking nothing of me.

"Are you ready to go home angel? I think George wants to close up." I lift my head and look into those piercing blue eyes and wonder why I got so lucky. He could have lost his shit seeing me crying over my cheating ex's baby news, but instead he has comforted me and allowed me head space. I don't ever want to lose him. I don't ever want to have to wake up without him by my side. Today has taught me one thing and that's to fight and protect what you truly want in life and with Max sat by my side I know now, no matter how much it hurts right now, I'm thankful that Josh did what he did. If he didn't, there is no way on earth that I would be sat in his arms right now.

"What time is it?" My voice is croaky from my tears and I probably look like no one owns me right now too.

"It's just past nine, angel."

"I'm so sorry Max. I know you had stuff that you needed to do. You should have gone back."

"Don't be silly. I'm not going to leave you, angel." Leaning down to press a soft kiss in my hair, he pulls back and looks straight into my eyes. "I need you to know one thing. I'm never, ever, going to leave you. No matter what the cost, no matter what the sacrifice. It's about time that I acted like a man and admitted that you come first. You'll always come first to me. I need you in my life and I'll keep you in my life whichever way I can get you."

I have no words to say to him. I'm filled with mixed emotions from today and there is so much that I want to say to him, but I physically can't do it. So instead I push forwards and pull his face down to mine, slowly yet desperately taking his lips in mine. Our kiss speaks so much more than our words ever could, and I try to tell him how thankful I am for him and how he has cared for me today. My loveable rogue giving up everything just so that I could be comforted by his presence, and that means more to me than he will ever know.

By the time we pull up outside my house all the lights are off. Either my mums in bed or she's gone out to only god knows where. Hopefully if it's the latter, she doesn't come back to make a scene, because I really don't think I could deal with that right now.

"How you holding up angel?" Max asks as his warm hand gives my thigh a reassuring squeeze. It's the first time he's asked me. I'm not sure if it's because he's been worried about my reaction, but his words are comforting to me.

"Better with you here." I smile a genuine smile at him to let him know that I'm telling him the truth. "Thank you for today."

"There isn't anything that I wouldn't do for you angel. You need to make sure you remember that and I'll tell you every day for the rest of our lives if I have too." He whispers as he leans over the console and kisses my forehead tenderly. I'm so glad he's here with me. We've been through so much since he came into my life and I don't think I will ever be able to express how much safer he makes me feel.

I notice my mum's shoes as we walk through the door. Good, at least she's still here and not causing mayhem somewhere else.

"Have you eaten today?" Max asks as we make our way further into the house. Come to think of it, I haven't and I don't think I could stomach anything right now either.

"I've not been hungry. I'm sure I'll be okay until tomorrow."

"You sure? I can always make you something before we go up if you want?"

"Honestly I'm fine." My fingers find their way into his hair as I look at him. "All I need right now is you." I'm scooped up into his strong arms and he wastes no time in carrying me up the stairs. Something has definitely changed between us today and I can only hope it's for the better.

I'm instantly pinned against the bedroom wall as

soon as we enter the bedroom, and in one swift motion Max kicks the door closed with his foot.

"Are you sure you want this, Jess?" Max asks with a seriousness to his voice. He looks at me intently as he waits for my answer.

"Definitely. I've wanted nothing else for weeks, Max. I'm fed up of pushing you away. I want us to go back to how we were before that cow wormed her way in and ruined it for us."

"No one has ruined anything Jess. You, you're all that I want. You're all that I *need*. Every goddamn fucking day." That's all I needed to hear as I pull him closer to me so I can feel him where I need him to be. My leg is pulled from underneath me as he wraps it firmly around his waist. I feel all the tension leave my body from his touch, as he roams his magical fingers from my thigh all the way up to my neck.

"I've missed this, I've missed us. I won't let anything keep you from me again."
A soft whimper escapes my lips as his hand works its way over the peak of my nipple. This is pure torture and he fucking knows it. Pressing my leg against him, he smiles against my lips and says, "I'm not rushing this Jess, I've waited far too long."
It's pointless fighting it. I know he'll just drag it out, purely just work me up more and more ,so I let him take full control of my body; desperate for the release that I know he will give me.

I don't let go of him as he carries me to the bed and he lays me down gently, acting as if a single touch would break me. I pull him down with me, not wanting the connection between us to be disturbed. Unable to hold back much longer, my hands sneak down to the bottom of his shirt as I try in desperation to open the buttons. Without a moment's hesitation, I grab the material in my both of my hands and rip his shirt open and slide it away from him revealing that perfectly toned torso that I like to admire so much. Max takes his sweet time removing the clothes from my body and when I'm finally just in my underwear he goes even slower.

"Max..." I moan. What is he trying to do to me? "Don't do this to me. I need you; please don't make me wait any longer." I can't help but plead to him. I feel like I'm about to combust at any moment. Both of my hands suddenly get entwined within his wrists as he pins them above my head.

"You're so fucking beautiful. I want to admire every goddamn part of you."

"Mmm. Why don't you explore every part of me instead?" He pulls back and looks at me with one eyebrow raised.

"Every part?"

"Every part, but that part." I say suddenly realising what I asked him and he laughs. Deciding enough is enough I push myself up now that his hands have relaxed against my wrists and push him back so that he's now the one lying down. I make quick work of removing his pants much to the growl that rumbles from his chest. I take him in my hands and slide up and down his length, while leaning in to tease him with my mouth. He buckles his hips at my touch, pleading for more and I feel a sudden urge of power course through me.

"But I want to admire every part of you." I mimic his words and he doesn't like it one bit. It has just the effect that I need, and he soon shoots up and pushes me back so that I'm lay down again. This time my underwear is removed and I can feel him pressing against my entrance. My hands cup his arse, as I impatiently wait for him to enter me and deciding enough is enough, I push him into me. I let out a cry of pleasure at the feel of him inside me after so long. He stills for a second and then he starts to move, thrusting into me to find our perfect rhythm as we move in sync with each other. I'm so close already and I can tell Max is almost there too, as I fell him stiffen inside me. Not wanting it to end, I press into him once more and cry out as my orgasm ripples through my body. Remembering that someone else is in the house, I bite down on Max's shoulder, hard, as I contract around him and after a few more forceful, yet pleasurable movements he reaches his climax with my name on his lips. We lie in each other's arms, sweaty and equally content as our breathing slowly calms down.

"You're something fucking else, Jessica Townsend. Do you know that?"

"Apparently so Mr Wild." I smile as I curl into him and feel the darkness wash over me.

Jess

"Are you shitting me? Why has it taken you so long to tell me?" I've been at Jens for an hour and I have just told her about the dramas of yesterday and now she's blowing steam out of her ears. "Fancy that little slag doing that when you're practically her boss. I always said she was weirdo, didn't I?"

I'm beginning to wish that I didn't bloody bring it up now. "There's nothing you can do to change it now, Jen. Flapping your arms around like a mad woman definitely won't make a difference." I know she means well and she's angry because I'm upset, but she's a bloody drama queen at times.

"What do you mean we can't do anything to change it? We can pissing rip his balls of so that he can't do it again. What a bastard, how can he even breed? I know it's not ideal, but at least you're out of that dead end relationship and on a major plus side, you bagged a right hottie not long after."

"Shhh, keep your voice down. I feel bad enough that I spent the whole day crying over my ex and how he's got his bit on the side pregnant, while he did nothing but comfort me and make sure that I was okay."

I look to the other side of the living room and watch Max and Luke catching up while being proper boys playing on the Xbox. I'm not going to lie, it's quite a sight and I love seeing this relaxed side to Max. If anyone were to see him now, they wouldn't expect him to carry the weight of his business issues on his shoulders and the mysterious darkness of his past that haunts him. All they would see is Max, as the fun loving twenty-nine year old guy that he really is underneath all of that hard, manly exterior.

As if sensing me watching him, he looks back at me over his shoulder and throws me a cheeky wink and I can't stop the school girl grin that takes over my face.

"I wasn't in the mood to talk much yesterday, Jen." I say as I look back towards my best friend.

"Come to think of it, that will probably explain why I haven't seen or heard from her recently. The little slags probably been avoiding me like the plague. Just you wait until I see her, the little cow, and don't even get me started on that twat."

"Fucking hell Jen, you're giving me a headache. He's a bastard, she's a home wrecking slut and as long as I don't have to work with her, then that's good enough for me."

"Oi, muscles." She shouts through to Max. "I fucking hope you gave him a beating of a lifetime when you saw him?"

"Believe me I wanted to, but I knew that would only upset Jess more. He's been warned to stay away from her. Next time he won't have such a lucky escape."

"Seriously? What's the point of you being built like a shit house, if you don't put it to good use?"

"Maybe you're best off asking Jess that question." He grins and I can't stop the girly laugh that comes out.

"You two are fucking animals." The look on her face is priceless as she scrunches her nose up.

"Err, hello. Pot. Kettle, black?" I ask but she remains quiet. "Yeah, I thought as much. You and Luke seem to be all right now. Did you tell him about your little drama?"

"Don't be so loud, jeez. Are you crazy? That's a little something that he doesn't need to find out about, like ever. Okay?"

"Well he's not going to hear it from me, is he? You need to tell him eventually though."

"Yeah, yeah, whatever." She shrugs. When they get serious, because they will, she's going to need to be as honest with him as she can be, because eventually this stuff has a wicked way of catching up with you and then what's she going to do apart from drown herself in a few bottles of wine when the shit hits the fan?

"What's happening with your mum?" She asks and I know that she's keen to change the subject. It's understandable if he's only in the room next door.

"Honestly? I have no idea. She seems okay at mine for now, but I've told her that it's not a permanent fixture and she needs to get herself a job and fast. If that works out then hopefully bit by bit we can get her life back together."

"Who knows, this might bring you closer together."

"Maybe." I'm still doubtful. I don't see how someone can change that drastically overnight, but I'm willing to give it ago.

"Right ladies, we've got to head out, but we'll be back later." Max leans in behind me and pulls me tight against him and I can't help but loose myself in him. "Do you need anything while I'm out?"

"Nope, I'm good I think. I'll text you if I think of anything."

"Fucking hell, is your phone actually on today?"

"Yep... I charged it last night and I don't want to think about all the messages that I have to get through."

"Maybe it will teach you to use it then." Slapping him playfully I reach up to meet his waiting lips. I don't think I could ever tire from them, or him for that matter. He's utterly and completely my personal addiction and there is no way that I ever want to come down from the high I

get when I'm around him.
"See you later."

Me and Jen spend the rest of the day lazing about watching crap on tele. I manage to tell her bits of my adventure from Australia, as I didn't get a chance to the other day and she thinks it's hilarious that Liss is so similar to her.

"Don't think you'll be replacing me when you go back, bitch. Trust me when I say that I will come and hunt you down."

"I said she's similar to you, not that she is you. It would be good to see how you get on though. Why don't you come over for a week or two when we fly back out? Come on it will be fun. I can show you how the other half live." Jen burst out laughing at me.

"Have you heard yourself you posh cow?"

"You'd fit right in. Just imagine being able to sunbathe all day when you know the weathers this shit over here."

"Yeah, you've got a good point there actually. Maybe I could even find my own Muscles while I'm over there. Now that would be fun."

"As long as you make sure you keep well away from my muscles, then we won't have a problem."

"Have you see how Max looks at you? He acts as if you're the only person to have a fucking vagina, so I think you'll be pretty safe. He's completely besotted with you."

"Oh piss off." I blush, suddenly feeling embarrassed. "Do you know what? I actually can't wait to get back over there. Hopefully Stella will do one eventually, now that would be the icing on the bloody cake."

"I'd love to meet her actually." Jen says and I can tell from the look on her face that she'd make sure it was a first impression that Stella wouldn't forget in a long while

Max

"Jess isn't here." I've been stood outside Jess' house in the pouring down rain for about ten minutes waiting for her mum to answer the fucking door.

"I know. I've just come back to do some stuff for her while she's catching up with Jen. So am I okay to come in?" She eyes me wearily, unsure whether or not to let *'delightful'* me into the house or not.

"Do I have a choice?" Her attitude in general is fucking horrible, but with me she likes turn it up a few notches and I have no fucking idea why.

"Not really. It's more of a surprise for her. You could always help me with it if you like?"

"What does she need a surprise for? It isn't her birthday and it sure as hell isn't any kind of special occasion."

I smile at the woman stood before me, who apparently created my angel and I see no resemblance between them whatsoever.

"I know. I just want to do something nice for her. Is that such a bad thing Diana?"

"Well I guess that all depends on whether or not you have a guilty conscience, doesn't it?" She pulls the door back to let me in and I turn to face her.

"I'm going to be completely honest with you. Yes I do have a guilty conscience and it's a pretty fucking massive one and do you want to know why? I'm guilty because I wasn't there for your daughter when she needed me, and the worst one? I'm guilty as hell for pushing her away, purely so I could stop myself from having to battle my own demons."

Diana doesn't say anything straight away, she just continues to look at me like I'm a fucking slug or something that's she's stood on, and it's starting to really piss me off.

"Well Max, that's pretty specific isn't it?"

"I guess you want to know why I am telling you all this when you quite clearly couldn't give a damn about me, and that's perfectly fine by me. But I will tell you this. The reason why I am doing this is simple. I'm very fond of your daughter and I've come to realise that I will do *everything* and *anything* to make her happy, no matter what obstacles stand in my way. It's clear that you're not a huge fan of me and that's cool, I get it, but from now, and for as long as she wants me to stay in her life, I'll make damn sure that I'll look after and provide her with the life that she deserves, and if that means surprising her for no particular reason then so be it."

A faint, but noticeable smile crosses her lips as soon as I've finished my little speech. "That's good enough for me Max. How about I stick the kettle on before you start whatever it is that you're planning?"

"Sounds pretty good to me, but I just need to grab some bits from the car. I won't be long." Fucking hell, she's definitely going to be hard work

.

"What is it that you're actually doing?" She asks as I walk back into the house with my arms brimming with flat cardboard boxes.

"Starting as she means to go on, by emptying all these negative reminders out of her life. I think we'll start with the main culprit first of all. What do you say?"

"Josh?" Her eyes grow wide.

"Got it in one."

"Have you spoken to her about this? I don't know if

she'll be too happy if she comes home and finds his stuff gone. Are you even sure she wants him out of her life? For all you know, she could be waiting for him to come walking back through that door for him to tell her that he made a huge mistake and he should never have left her in the first place, yada yada."

I struggle to understand what she's saying. Did I just hear that right? She seems to be under the impression that Josh just upped and left one day. This is some crazy, crazy shit. But it's not my place to say. That alone lies with Jess. One thing I won't do is break her trust by setting her mother straight.

I've just about finished the front room when Diana comes back in to check on my progress.

"You'll end up hurting her you know. Guys like you always do."

JESS

It feels like any other weekend at Jens. Me and Jen have been sat on the sofa, curled up in our blankets watching re-runs of home and away. The only thing missing is George, but seeing as he is on a hot, smoking date that he wouldn't dream of cancelling, we decided to go ahead and watch them anyway. As I'm so far behind, Jen's having to watch most of them again.

"Quit moaning." I say to her. "If you weren't so impatient, then we both could have been watching these now for the first time."

"What was I supposed to do? A bunch of cheap knock off tests told me that I was going to be mum. How else am I expected to deal with the idea of spawning another me? Come on Jess, you would have done the fucking same, and you know it."

"Don't even think that you're going be milking that for the next nine months, because I will actually leave you for good."

"That's fine; I'm used to you gallivanting off at the drop of your knickers anyway."

"Hey, you cheeky bitch. That's a bit below the belt, even for you. You're the only one who casually drops your knickers not me."

"Yes but I'm proud of it baby." She laughs. "Oh hang on a sec, let me grab this." She leans over to grab her phone. "Hey lover boy. You missing me already?" I can't help but make gagging actions towards her. "Oh yeah I love the sound of that baby. You can strip me anytime. Surely you should know that you don't even need to ask."

"You're such a dirty bitch." I shout as she parades around the living room.

"Of course. I'll speak to you later."

"Quit looking at me like that. Don't tell me you and muscles don't have the odd bit of phone sex every now and again."

"Erm, we haven't actually. So come one then, what did Mr Lover, Lover want? I can tell that you're bursting at the seams to tell me."

"Oh, nothing important princess. I guess he just kind of makes me happy."

"I can tell when you're lying to me you know, but it's okay because two can play that game." It's okay, because the next time she wants some gossip; she's really going to have to work for it.

"Oh quite your moaning, woman." Jen says as she throws herself back down beside me.

"Stick the tele back on then" Feeling ready to throw something at her, I manage to hold back and turn my attention back to the screen."

"You've changed."

"What me?" I ask, unsure what she means.

"Yes, you. Normally you'd be pestering me until I told you everything."

"Piss off Jen. If you're not going to tell me then you're not going to tell me." I keep my eyes trained on the tele, knowing full well that she will break soon enough. *Why beg for it, when it can be handed to you on a shiny plate?* I think to myself. She will tell me eventually, even if it kills her. She's bloody shocking when it comes to keeping secrets

.

"What's going to happen once you have finished on the development?" We've just finished all of our unwatched episodes of home and away when I turn to look at her quizzically.

"What do you mean?"

"Well you know… you and Max. How will you still see each other?"

"I honestly don't know. He asked me to move in with him on a permanent basis."

"Why the fuck am I only just hearing about this now?" She dramatically jumps up from the sofa with her eyes bulging out of their sockets. "Holy shit Jess. Are you going to say yes?"

"I've told him that I can't just give up everything I have ever known to move in with him. I can't just up and leave, Jen.

"Why the hell not?"

"Fucking hell. If you wanted to get rid of me so badly, you could have just said." I stick my bottom lip out at her for added effect.

"Don't be so bloody stupid, you silly mare. All I am saying is that you should give it a try. If it doesn't work out, you've always got me and George to come back to."

"My home is here, Jen. My work is here. Everything that I want, except Max is here. I'm not prepared to give it all up just for it to fail. I physically and emotionally can't do it, Jen."

"You won't know unless you give it a try, princess."

"Come on, this is me that we're talking about. It's always going to go tit's up." Does she forget that she has been with me for most of my life? She's bloody witnessed every single fall that I've ever had, and none of them have been pretty. I won't be able to survive a fall this big if she isn't here beside me. Even then, I'm not completely sure I'll get over it fully.

"I personally think you should go for it. Whatever the outcome, I'll be here for you one hundred percent and you know this."

"I know." I mumble and glance at the clock. I'm surprised to see that it's already past seven. I wonder where Max and Luke have got to. It was only past noon when they left earlier. Maybe they've both come to their senses and realised that me and Jen might be a bit too much to handle. "Did Luke say what time those two were coming back?"

"He didn't say. I don't think they'll be much longer now. How about we crack open a bottle while we wait for those deliciously hot men of ours to return?" She doesn't need to ask me twice and before long, we're both settled back on the sofa, wine glass in hand waiting for our pizza to arrive."

MAX

Luke turns up with his van right on time. I started to
think that maybe he'd got lost or disappeared back to
Jens without me. I run down the stairs to let him in,
mainly to prevent the mass interrogation that he'll face
from Jess' mum. Fortunately it seems that she's took
herself out for a while. Good fucking riddance I say, all
I've heard from her today is *"Why are you doing this?
Why are you doing that?"* It's fucking draining as hell.

"What's taken you so long?" I ask as he rushes
through the door to get out of the down pour outside.

"There's been some kind of accident I think. All the
roads are backed up. I was at a standstill for an hour at
one point, mate."

"Well you're here now. Did you get everything that I
needed?" He nods at me and points to the van.
"Fucking perfect. How about we get started then, hey?"

Suddenly realising the time, I quickly dig out my
phone and give Jess a call to make sure she's okay.
I've not heard from her all day. As usual it takes her a
while to answer. How far away from the phone does
she need to be?

"Hi." She smiles down the line.

"Hey, angel. Listen I'm sorry that I've ditched you all
day, I've just had some stuff that needed sorting. I
shouldn't be too long now though."

"Cool. I did wonder what had happened to you." As
she talks, I slowly look around me and hope that I
haven't done the wrong thing.

"I bet you've been having fun though?"

"Yep. I'm all caught up on my Home and Away now, Jen's just fed and watered me and you can't go wrong with a bit of gossip thrown in." She sounds so happy to be back with her friends. The look on her face when she is with them is priceless and I can see why she would never want to leave them. This six monthly plan of Mal's is looking more promising, now more than ever.

"Well I'm just finishing up here and then I'll be coming to get you."
"I can't wait. See you soon."

"What the fucks happened to you, man?" Luke walks into the room as I finish my call. "I never thought I would see the day when you'd be getting all soft over a woman. I need to record this shit so I can make sure it's real."
"Piss off." I spit back at him and throw the rag his way. "What's going down with you and Jen? You're normally onto your next victim by now."
"Ah mate I wish I could tell you, really I do, but I don't know myself. What I do know is that she's smoking hot and she's fun to be around. There's never a dull moment between us."
"Just make sure you don't fuck her over Luke. If you're only being casual, make sure as hell that she's fully aware of it before she becomes attached to you. You know me mate. Normally I wouldn't get involved but it's Jess' best mate and if Jen gets hurt then Jess gets hurt too and I won't be able to sit back and watch that shit. She means too much to me. "
"Chill out man. There's no need to get all deep and shit on me, we're *both* just having some fun and enjoying each other's company. Why throw in some added pressure when you don't need to? Plus, you know I'm not the type of guy to fuck her over. One thing

about me, is that I'm always upfront. You of all people should know that."

Jess

One bottle has turned into three by the time Max and Luke have finally arrived back to Jen's. We're currently in the middle of a game of monopoly and shit is getting pretty heated between me and Jen, because I am winning her hands down and she doesn't like it one little bit.

"So this is what girls really get up to when they're left alone." Max says as he crouches down beside me. "You've not seen anything until you've witnessed one of us officially lose. It's not a pretty sight."

"It's true. I'm nothing but a sore loser." I giggle while looking at Max sat beside me. "I kind of missed you while you were gone." I whisper to him.

"I missed you too, angel. Any time away from you is too long, but I'm here now. I'll always be here, no matter what." He leans in and kisses the top of my head and I let out a sigh of contentment. "Just let me know when you want to go home angel."

All the lights are off when we pull up outside my house. "Guess my mum must have gone to bed early again."

"I meant to say, I called before and she wasn't here."

"Shit. I told her to stay here so I could keep an eye on her. I knew she'd bloody do this eventually." She couldn't even last a couple of days could she?

"Maybe she's popped in to see one of her friends or something. I'm sure she's old enough to look after herself, Jess."

To someone who doesn't know my mum or her

history, I can see why they would think I am overreacting, but I know her and I know this is the start of another spiral.

"She hasn't got any friends Max, at least not if you don't count the bottle. She's not here by choice, she's here because she had nowhere else to go. Looks like she's just blown that final chance with me anyway." I pull my keys out of my bag, suddenly unsure of what I am supposed to do now.

"I'll have a drive around and see if I can see her about. "

"Thank you Max. Are you sure you don't mind?" He shakes his head at me and I lean over to thank him with a kiss.

"I don't know what I have done to deserve you, but whatever it is, I'm grateful." I'm pulled in tighter into his embrace and the feel of his warm hard body sends tingles of pleasure to course through my body.

"It's me that doesn't deserve you, angel. Always remember that."

I reluctantly pull myself away from him and unfasten my seatbelt. "You might be out there looking for her, for some time. I don't even know if she's familiar with the places around here to be honest, and she doesn't even have a phone."

"Don't worry about it. I'll try and find her. You head inside and get warm, if she turns up while I'm out just call me okay?"

I wait until Max drives off before opening my door. I'm going to fucking strangle that so called mother of mine. I told her I wasn't going to put up with any of this funny business and what does she do? She drives me fucking crazy.

As I make my way through the house, I think how

dramatically my life has changed for the better since I caught Josh doing the dirty on me. It's crazy how much my life has taken a huge turn for the better and every now and then it completely blows me away. I've seen so many beautiful places in a few short weeks, that only people get to dream of. I wander into the kitchen and stop dead as I see my mum slumped over the side of the sofa out of the corner of my eye. I look next to her and see an empty bottle of vodka with a few pills lying on the table.

"Oh fuck." I scream. "Mum, mum can you hear me?" Oh shit, no. What has she done? I try to shake her gently but I get no response from her. "Mum, fucking answer me." Finally my brain registers that I need to get help. Grabbing the phone from the side I try to call emergency services, but as my hands are too clammy, the phone falls to the floor. When I eventually get a grip on the goddamn thing, I wait for someone to help me.

"I need an ambulance now. It's my mum, she's took an overdose." The words barely get passed the lump that has formed in my throat. I do my best to answer the questions that the operator asks me, but I struggle to concentrate as I see my mum lying before me all limp and lifeless. "Yes, she's breathing but barely. No, she's not responding to me at all. I need someone to get here as soon as they can before it's too late."

The ambulance turns up within five minutes of me ending the call and my mum is still unconscious. She seemed perfectly fine when I left her this morning. We even managed to have a proper conversation, something that we haven't done in a long time. Why would she do something like this? I'll always be the first to admit that we rarely see eye to eye, but surely she could have tried to talk to me before doing something so bloody stupid?

"Miss Townsend we need to get your mother to hospital."

"I'm coming with you." There is no way that I am leaving her side until I know that she is going to be alright.

On the way up to the hospital it suddenly dawns on me that Max is still out there somewhere looking for her.

"Max it's me. " I stutter through my tears. No matter what I do or how hard I try to stop them, they continue to fall.

"What's happened?" he asks, his voice urgent down the line.

"It's… it's my mum. She was in the house when I got in."

"Where are you? I can hear sirens."

"We're in the ambulance on the way to the hospital. Max I'm scared." I whimper. I can't lose her.

"Which one? I'm coming to you." I have to think for a moment unsure of which one is closest.

"The University college hospital." I reply and all of a sudden the line goes flat.

No sooner have we pulled up outside the hospital and the back doors swing open. It all feels like everything is happening in slow motion as my mum is wheeled away from the ambulance and rushed through the doors to the hospital. I'm told to wait in the waiting room and I have no idea where they are taking her, or how long they will be. All I can do is wait.

"Please be okay, please be okay." is all that runs through my head and I pray that the more I say it, then the more likely someone will hear it and answer me. I don't even know how long she was lay there for. I dread to think how much worse it could have been if I had have stayed at Jens much longer. What if I went with

Max to look for her? We could have been gone for hours trying to track her down. Just when everything in my life was righting itself, again in the blink of an eye something happens to make it all come crashing down again.

"Jess." I hear my name being called out in the distance and I slowly lift my head up and turn in that direction. Max comes rushing to my side and takes my tear stained face into his hands.

"Hey, shhh. Please don't cry, angel."

"What am I going to do? I could have stopped this from happening." I whimper into his chest as he holds me close. "This is all my fault. She tried to take her own life for fucks sake. How did I not see this coming?"

MAX

"Has anyone been to tell you what's happening? You've been sat here for ages." She shakes her head against my chest unable to form words through her pain. I feel her shudder beneath me and there's not a fucking thing I can do about it, apart from hold her for as long as she will allow me to do so.

This is absolute bollocks. Why has she been sat out here on her own with no one telling her what's happening? "I'm going to see what I can find out. Will you be okay here for a moment? I stand and lean down to place a kiss on her head before I set off to reception.

"Excuse me. Could you please tell me if there has been an update on Diana Townsend yet?"

"And you are?" The snotty brunette before me asks, while looking down her nose at me. Seriously in a place like this, is it that fucking hard to use some manners?

"I'm her son-in-law and I'd like an update." I snap but to be honest, I'm beyond pissed off right now.

"The doctors are with her at the moment. As soon as they have an update, they will be out to let you know. "

"Thank you." I say through gritted teeth. I fucking hate not being able to do anything. Jess is sat here absolutely heartbroken and there's nothing that I can do to erase that pain for her, and to make it worse I fucking hate sitting around in hopsitals, fear gripping you every time a door swings open knowing that it could be bad news that waits for you.

"Here you go." I say to Jess as I pass her a plastic

cup filled with cheap and bitter coffee and I get the tiniest smile from her.

"Thank you." She sips at silently for a while and then says, "I should have put my foot down more with her. Maybe I should have demanded that she needed to see someone the other day when I realised that her drinking was getting out of control."

"Jess, baby. There is no way you could have predicted that this was going to happen. Don't you dare start blaming yourself because that will just make me angry. She'll be fine, just you wait and see." I hate myself instantly as soon as those words leave my lips. I have no right promising her something that I have absolutely no control over. I'll do anything I can to remove that heartbroken look from her face and to ease her pain away.

"Ms Townsend." A tall doctor approaches us and I'd say he was mid-forties at the most. As he stands before us he removes his glasses and looks at her with a stern expression. Oh shit, this doesn't look good at all. "Your mother is very lucky to be alive. I'd say had you found her no more than thirty to forty five minutes later; there is an excessively high chance that things could have taken a severe turn for the worst."

"Oh my god. Is she going to be okay?"

"We've managed to wake her, but she isn't really in a position to talk at the moment. She's stable, but we should know more tomorrow once we have run some extra tests to see what kind of damage has been done, but at this moment in time everything looks how we want it to. If you and you're husband would like to come back in the morning? I think your mother will be more responsive once her body has gotten over the shock."

"Yes. Of course, thank you."

"Thank you." I say to the doctor. I know Jess isn't

going to be happy about leaving her, but she needs some rest too.

Jess remains quite on the drive home and I don't press her. She'll talk to me when she wants to. I'd be a fucking hypocrite if I started demanding answers from her, after I pushed her away with Mal. I'll show her that I can be here for her no matter what she needs. As soon as we enter the house, Jess makes her way straight upstairs while I tidy up the mess that her mother left lying round. First of all I clear up the pills that are scattered around the coffee table, and discard of the empty vodka bottle. Her mum must be in a really bad place for her to even think of doing such a thing. I just hope that Jess doesn't close herself off because of this. She blames herself and I don't understand why. Maybe she'll open up to me when she's ready

.

"Did you do this?" She asks as I enter the bedroom. She stands in front of me and then spins around in the room. After the events of tonight, I'd completely forgotten about my surprise for her.

"Yes." I say as I walk over to her. "I hope you don't mind?"

"Do I hell. I bloody love it."

"I thought if you were making a fresh start then you'd prefer to be out with the old and in with the new." Reaching out, I place my hands around her and pull her into me. "Whatever you need, whatever you want, I will always make sure you get it."

"Well what I want right now is curl up with you in my nice new bed." She smiles at me and it's bloody hard to resist her. She's everything and more that I never knew I needed, until she came crashing into my life and I'm so glad she did.

"Thank you, for everything." She whispers, as I feel

her curl up against me, her soft silky skin pressing against me, completing me and chipping more ice away from my damaged heart.

"I hate that you've had to suffer so much angel in such a short time, but the more that I think about it, the more I'm thankful that you did. If it hadn't have been for you finding out about that cheating son of a bitch, I don't think we'd be where we are now. But let me tell you this, I will make sure that I treasure you right up to my dying breath and I will never, ever allow anyone to hurt you or treat you that way again." As I say it, I have never been so sure of anything in my life. This little angel of mine will never want for anything as long as I am around.

"Your coffee is on the side. I'm going to grab a quick shower before we set off okay?" Jess looks a lot better now that she's managed to get some sleep. I spent most of the night watching her and wondering how I got so fucking lucky to get to have her in my life. I hear my phone ringing from the bedside table. Heath's name dances at me from the caller I.D and I answer it instantly.

"Hey mate, it's me."

"What's taking so long?" How hard can it be to search a fucking computer? I hope my suspicions aren't right. It's been playing on my mind for a couple of days now and I really need to know.

"Well the files are there all right and so is a lot of other sensitive information. The worrying thing is that it's not just on the PC, it's all saved to Jess's account."

"Fuck. Heath I need you to pull me the CCTV footage from the past two weeks. Watch it if you have to, but make sure you tell me exactly what you find on there, whether I'm going to like it or not. You hear me?"

"You got it. I'll call you as soon as I know more."

"I want everything in Jess' office searched and reported back to me ASAP." My body's shaking when I get off the phone. I need to know what the whole point of this is. Why would someone drop super sensitive files on to Jess' computer for it to look like she's stealing the business' details when she has them already. I have a pretty good idea, but I need it clarifying before I can do anything about it.

"You ready angel?" I ask. I find her sat on the sofa staring into space. "Hey."

"Umm. Yeah, I guess. I'm just worried about what's going to happen when I get there. I don't think I can cope with facing her Max."

"I'll be beside you all the way, and if when we get there you find it's getting too much all you have to do is tell me and we'll go okay?"

"She needs to get help Max. Ever since my dad left, she's never been the same and now after losing the house and her job, I think it's all gotten too much for her."

"We'll make sure she gets the best care that money can buy if she needs it. You just tell me what you need and I'll do the rest angel."

We don't stay too long at the hospital. I made Jess go in on her own at first so she could talk to her mum in private, but she wouldn't even look at Jess. All she did was stare at the ceiling. I managed to speak to the doctor in charge of her care to see what type of treatment she will need when she is ready to be discharged, but apparently it's too early to tell. Whatever it is that she needs, I made a promise to Jess to make sure she gets it and as soon as I know, I'll make sure that it gets it arranged.

"Hey." I answer on the first ring. I pray that Heath isn't about to tell me what I think he is. I walk out of the bedroom so that I don't disturb Jess while she has a nap. All this with her mum has well and truly taken it out of her.

"Okay, I think we have finally gotten to the bottom of it. Are you sat down' because you're not going to like this at all Max."

"Just hurry up and tell me what I already suspect." I bark down the phone.

"Okay, fine, I've had a look at the CCTV footage over the past two weeks and everyday Stella has been going into Jess' office, constantly messing around with her computer."

"Fuck," I shout. I fucking knew it, deep down, I knew.

"That's not all. There are few calls that have been made to a British number from your office over the past couple of weeks too. I'm sorry mate. I'm not sure what she's trying to achieve, but whatever it is, it seems pretty dodgy to me. Maybe try and catch her out? What do you want me to do from this end?"

"Cheers mate. Keep your eye on her for me? I know exactly what she's trying to do. She's trying to stitch Jess up and I won't fucking put up with it. Actually, when you see her, get her to call me as soon as she can." It's time I think like Jess and see how I can trip her up and hopefully I'll get to the bottom of this bullshit once and for all.

ACKNOWLEDGEMENTS

I always worry when I write acknowledgements that I will end up missing people off. If I do, I sincerely apologise.

Firstly I would like to thank the Mr once again for allowing me to ignore him while I go into my own little bubble to write and supplying me with obscene amounts of coffee as requested. It really means a lot and I will never be able to put into words how thankful I am for your support.

To all the fabulous bloggers who work tirelessly sharing, taking part in cover reveals etc. The promotions that you do are outstanding and I am grateful to each and every one of you that take the time out of your day to endlessly share my posts, sales etc. You are absolutely amazing.

To Justine, Charisse, Victoria, Jade, Diana, Tracey and all of my lovely ladies, thank you also for your continued support. I love hearing from you and reading your reviews. You lovelies are one in a million to me.

I have loved diving back into Max and Jess' world once again. There is never a dull moment with this bunch, that's for sure.

Thank you to my readers. I can't thank you enough for the support you give me. It makes me really happy to know that you love Jess and Max just as much as me.

About the Author:

Welcome to the crazy and hectic life that is me...
A fun, loving mum of one special little boy, girlfriend (I'm
sure it should be wife by now!!) and an overall crazy,
happy go lucky girl from England.

I have always had a passion for reading and writing.
Wherever I am, my book reader is never far behind
along with a mug of coffee.

I found myself wanting to write from a young age, I
have quite a few hidden stories on my computer
somewhere, maybe I will have to dig them out and play
around with them at some point.

I decided to make the very exciting but also very nerve
wracking decision to release my debut 'Escape down
under' at the end of 2013 when the ideas in my head
got too strong and just wouldn't leave me alone.

Follow S.M Phillips:

www.facebook.com/sphillipsauthor

www.twitter.com/s_m_phillips_

11541014R00123

Printed in Great Britain
by Amazon.co.uk, Ltd.,
Marston Gate.